Cassidy C

Once, in Belgium, a flawless blue diamond had caught his eye. He'd seen it lying there against a background of black velvet and the sensation that gripped him had been so visceral, so singular and paralyzing that it transcended mere desire. He'd looked at it, and he'd known he had to have it.

He looked at Savannah now, with the wind whipping her long gold hair and the candlelight glowing and flickering on her face. He heard the soft husky sound of her laughter, saw the sparks in her eyes, and it was Belgium all over again.

He knew he was lost.

Dear Reader:

Welcome to Silhouette Desire – provocative, compelling, contemporary love stories written by and for today's woman. These are stories to treasure.

Each and every Silhouette Desire is a wonderful romance in which the emotional and the sensual go hand in hand. When you open a Desire, you enter a whole new world – a world that has, naturally, a perfect hero just waiting to whisk you away! A Silhouette Desire can be light-hearted or serious, but it will always be satisfying.

We hope you enjoy this Desire today – and will go on to enjoy many more.

Please write to us:

Jane Nicholls
Silhouette Books
PO Box 236
Thornton Road
Croydon
Surrey
CR9 3RU

Stealing Savannah
DONNA CARLISLE

*First published in Great Britain in 1994
by Silhouette Books, Eton House, 18-24 Paradise Road,
Richmond, Surrey TW9 1SR*

© Donna Ball 1994

*Silhouette, Silhouette Desire and Colophon are
Trade Marks of Harlequin Enterprises B.V.*

ISBN 0 373 59309 0

22-9409

Made and printed in Great Britain

DONNA CARLISLE

lives in Atlanta, Georgia, with her teenage daughter. Weekends and summers are spent in her rustic north Georgia cabin, where she enjoys hiking, painting and planning her next novel.

Donna has also written under the pseudonyms Rebecca Flanders and Leigh Bristol.

Other Silhouette Books by Donna Carlisle

Silhouette Desire

Under Cover
A Man Around the House
Interlude
Matchmaker, Matchmaker
For Keeps
The Stormriders
Cast Adrift
It's Only Make Believe

One

With a passkey lifted from the pocket of a maid he had bumped into in the hall, C. J. Cassidy silently let himself into the penthouse suite, crossed the room in the dark and helped himself to over a thousand dollars in cash, a gold initial ring and a Rolex watch. Without ever disturbing the room's sleeping occupant, he returned to the corridor and rode down to the lobby on the elevator. At three o'clock in the morning, he had the elevator to himself.

The lobby of the elegant Boheme Hotel was similarly deserted. Cassidy stepped off the elevator and concealed himself behind an enormous planter of cascading greenery, pretending to study a directory while he waited to see if anyone would come to the desk. No one did, and he strolled casually toward the exit.

Then he stopped, his eyes caught by a discreet brass plaque that read Offices. He'd already emptied the hotel safe of everything worth taking—and he was forever amazed by the worthless items people felt compelled to lock away in a safe while leaving things like cash and jewelry lying about on their night tables.

He moved down the corridor toward the offices.

The first door he tried was unlocked, which was suspicious enough in itself. He opened it a crack and saw the darkened outer office was deserted, but a faint stream of light was coming from the half-open door beyond it. Cassidy stepped inside and closed the door silently behind him.

On his way across the room, he effortlessly picked the lock on the secretary's desk and liberated a set of keys and the contents of the petty cash box. The reception area opened onto several other offices, the doors to all of which were closed and locked—except one.

The door from which the small pool of light escaped was marked Assistant Manager, and in smaller letters, S. Monterey. Cassidy pushed it open slowly and very carefully.

A small lamp cast a circle of yellow light over the desk but left the rest of the room in shadows. It was just as well, for C.J.'s attention, in those first crucial moments after entering the room, was completely riveted on the desk—and the exquisite creature who was asleep there.

Her head was resting on the desk, cushioned by one slender, outstretched arm. A cascade of fine, pale gold hair curtained her shoulders and cast a gentle half-crescent shadow over her face. Her porcelain-white skin reminded him of a painting by one of the old masters, so delicate and translucent that it seemed to be illuminated by another worldly source.

A faint sleep-flush tinged her cheeks pink, and beneath the veil of her eyelids he could see the soft movement of dreams. Her lashes were dark and tipped with gold, resting like feathery wings against her cheek. Her lips were unpainted, slightly parted with the soft, even rhythm of her breath, a smooth natural flesh-pink that was delicately moistened at the corners. The arm on which she rested her head was her left one; the fingers were slender and graceful like the rest of her, slightly curved in the relaxed posture of sleep.

Her fingernails were manicured into a curved feminine shape and decorated with a frosty flesh-colored polish; she wore no rings at all. A small watch on a cameo bracelet was her only ornamentation, and it suited her perfectly.

An angel, C.J. thought, and for one long and thoroughly enjoyable moment he was completely entranced. In his profession he often came upon the unexpected, but few surprises were as pleasant as this. He had done a good night's work; he rewarded himself by allowing a few moments to simply drink in the scene.

But as he stood there, bemused by the shape of her softly parted lips, the half-moon shadows her lashes cast on her cheekbones, the silken fall of hair, he was tantalized by an impulse that he knew immediately would be impossible to resist. Since entering the hotel twenty-eight minutes ago, C. J. Cassidy had stolen eight thousand dollars in cash, jewelry worth another ten thousand, the security code, computer passwords and restricted files by several key departments, along with enough miscellaneous credit cards, keys and checkbooks to disrupt their owners' lives for weeks to come. Why not add a kiss to the list?

He crossed as silently as a panther to the desk, and stood behind the light so that not even the shadow of his presence would disturb her. Once he had been known to have the lightest touch in the business; he could divest a man of his watch or his wallet in the time it would take someone else to think about it, and be gone in a heartbeat, leaving not a trace to mark his passing. He took his kiss in the same way. As smooth as a whisper, he leaned over her. Her scent, warm and faintly humid and tinged with jasmine, enveloped him. With the very tips of his fingers, he lifted a strand of hair away from her face and bent his head to hers.

It was more of a blending of breaths than a touch, an inhaling of essence, a slow delicious savoring of promise, as rich with sensual appeal as the moment one first tastes a fine rare wine, letting its aroma sink into the pores and intoxicate before the first drop is drunk. He could feel his pulse pound as he moved closer, for the risk was great and the danger an essential part of the excitement. He parted his lips and pressed them over hers lightly, so lightly it was more of a thought than a deed. With the tip of his tongue he tasted her, caressed her, and by the time she stirred, sighing a little in her sleep and shifting her head more comfortably on her arm, he was gone.

Savannah disentangled herself from the shroud of a strangely erotic dream with great reluctance. She was not usually the type to linger in slumber or become befuddled by dreams; when she awoke, she did so with a clear head and instant awareness, no matter what time of the day or night it might be. She knew, for example, even now, that she had fallen asleep at her desk approximately three hours ago and that she really needed to wake up and go home before the morning staff found her like this. And that was exactly what she intended to do, but she had been working sixteen-hour days for the last two weeks and she was exhausted; she deserved a few more moments to linger in the pleasant glow of the dream, to taste the warmth of his kiss on her lips. As soft as the press of a petal against her flesh, yet heated with an underlying strength barely restrained, tasting of wintergreen and a definite, distinctive masculinity...

Savannah opened her eyes and there he was, rifling through her filing cabinet.

Her heart gave such a lurch of alarm that for a moment she couldn't even react. There was a strange man in her office at three o'clock in the morning and it was obvious he was up to no good. Yet all she could think about was how tall he was, how appealingly his dark hair curled over the back of his white turtleneck and what an attractive picture his slim figure presented from behind.

Over the turtleneck, he wore a casually cut silk jacket and European-style trousers of a similar fabric. His hands were long-fingered and lithe as they moved silently over her file folders, and for the longest moment Savannah couldn't seem to drag her eyes away from those hands. She felt again the brush of a fingertip cross her cheek and tasted wintergreen on her lips.

But that was ridiculous. In the past three weeks, there had been half a dozen burglaries in the hotel and she was very possibly looking at the man responsible for them. She kept her purse in that file drawer, and it had been locked when she fell asleep.

Even as she watched, he found her purse and opened it, and Savannah was galvanized into action. In a single motion, she pushed away from the desk and lunged for the only semblance of a weapon the room offered—a brass umbrella stand by the door. Snatching it up like a club, she declared, "All right, mister. Hold it right there. Now turn around. Slowly."

He did so.

His coal black hair was brushed away from a high forehead, his cheekbones were sharp, his lips full, his eyes smoky gray. His lower face was shadowed by the ghost-beard that was common to many dark-haired men and—in Savannah's opinion at least—added approximately thirty points to his sex appeal, which was already well above average. A hint of a rueful smile deepened one corner of his lips and he leaned his shoulder against the file cabinet with a negligent ease that managed to look both endearing and insolent.

"Curses, foiled again," he said mildly. "And here I was planning to leave you as silently as I came, with nothing more than sweet dreams to remind you of our brief encounter."

Savannah swallowed hard. Surely he couldn't mean...he wouldn't have...she had only *dreamed* that kiss. Hadn't she?

"Who are you?" she demanded. "What are you doing here?"

The rueful smile deepened. "That would seem rather obvious, wouldn't it? At the moment, I appear to have been caught in the act and am being held at bay by a woman wielding a weapon of..." He cast a faint puzzled glance toward the umbrella stand, and finished simply, "indeterminate origin. At the very least, the graceful exit I had planned is completely spoiled. At the most..." Again he cast a dubious glance toward the umbrella stand. "Well, while I wouldn't exactly call that a deadly weapon, I would venture to say you could do some serious damage with that thing if you put your mind to it. And I'd say that just about sums up my situation, wouldn't you?"

For a moment, Savannah just stared at him, fighting the lure of his sensuous, mesmerizing voice. He certainly didn't sound like a burglar, or look like one, for that matter—as though she would know what a burglar was supposed to look or sound like. Still, she wanted to believe the best. Flexing her fingers around the base of the umbrella stand, she demanded cautiously, "What were you doing with my purse?"

He lifted an eyebrow. "Trying to steal it, of course."

And that eliminated whatever doubts she might have had. Her heart began to thump rapidly again. So here she was, having single-handedly captured a self-confessed criminal, alone in her office at three o'clock in the morning with nothing between herself and disaster except a brass umbrella stand, and what was she supposed to do now?

Savannah eyed the telephone on the desk a good four feet away from where she stood, then looked back at him. Again she tested the weight of the object in her hands, but who was she kidding? All he had to do was walk past her and out the door; she couldn't stop him unless she attacked him in cold blood and that was something she knew herself to be completely incapable of doing.

The trick was to make sure *he* didn't know that.

"Stay right there," she warned him, edging toward the desk and hoping her voice sounded steely edged and threatening. "Don't move."

"Wouldn't think of it," he murmured, his expression perfectly bland.

She reached the desk without taking her eyes off him, but then came the tricky part—balancing the umbrella stand in one hand while trying to hold the receiver to her ear and dial with the other hand, and all without losing her tentative advantage over the criminal who lounged so casually against the filing cabinet across from her. With less grace than determination, she managed the maneuver and punched out the three digits that would connect her with the security office.

The phone was answered on the second ring, and relief left Savannah's knees weak.

She did not let that show in her voice, however, as she snapped out, "This is Savannah Monterey. I've captured an intruder in my office. Get a security team up here right away. And call the police."

The intruder lifted a finger to attract her attention. Such was his natural air of command that Savannah actually waited to hear what he had to say.

"And the manager," he suggested. "Don't forget to give him a call. He'll want to be in on this."

Greg Walker, the hotel manager, lived in the penthouse and was accustomed to being awakened in the middle of the night for emergencies. Savannah herself had never called him for one, but she had never had an emergency like this before. And it was true— Greg Walker would want to be notified immediately of this development.

Without taking her eyes off the man on the other side of the room, she said into the telephone, "Ring Mr. Walker's suite and tell him what's happened. And get someone over here *now*."

She dropped the receiver into its cradle and backed away from the desk. Suddenly, the eight feet of carpet and three feet of desk that separated her from the dark-haired criminal did not seem to be enough. He smiled and glanced at his watch, marking the time. Savannah noticed with narrowing eyes that it appeared to be a very expensive watch. And what kind of burglar could afford an Italian-cut silk jacket, anyway?

The answer came back to her with mocking overtones of logic: A very good one.

It was then that she noticed he kept the fingers of his right hand closed, obviously hiding something. A weapon? Or more likely her wallet? After all, his hands had last been in her purse.

"What have you got in your hand? What are you hiding?"

He opened his fingers and glanced at the contents as though he'd forgotten what he was holding.

"You stole that from my purse, didn't you?" she declared, outrage rising.

He gave her an utterly enchanting smile. "Guilty," he confessed. "Would you like it back?"

"Put it on the desk," Savannah ordered. Instinctively, she took a step back as he approached. "And don't try anything funny."

Very carefully, moving with exaggerated deliberation, he placed the pilfered object on the edge of her desk. It was a foil-wrapped chocolate kiss. Savannah always kept a handful of them in her purse in case of an emergency; she was something of a chocolate addict and didn't like to risk being too far away from the source of her greatest comfort.

She raised her gaze from the incriminating evidence of her weakness to his dancing eyes, and a peculiar tingling feeling attacked the pit of her stomach. She supposed he couldn't help it if he didn't look like a criminal, but for heaven's sake, why couldn't he at least *act* like one?

The wicked amusement in his eyes charged the air with an expectation that was entirely inappropriate, and the moment between them went on far too long. When she heard the noise in the hall, it was all she could do to keep from sighing out loud.

The door to the receptionist's office burst open and a voice shouted, "Ms. Monterey! Are you all right?"

The burglar glanced at his watch again. "Two minutes, twenty-seven seconds," he murmured. "I can't say I like that."

Savannah tore her scowling gaze from him to the outer office and answered, "In here! Hurry, for heaven's sake!"

He said, "Ms. Monterey, is it? I assure you, you are in no—"

But he very wisely broke off and stepped back when the door was flung open and two uniformed men burst in. When he saw they held guns, he—also very wisely—lifted his hands to the height of his shoulders.

Savannah lowered the heavy umbrella stand to the floor with profound relief and leaned against the wall weakly.

"Are you all right, ma'am? Are you hurt?"

She allowed herself one moment to reflect upon how much danger she might have been in and another moment to compose herself. Then she straightened her shoulders and replied briskly, "I'm fine. I think we've caught our burglar, gentlemen. This man broke in here—"

"The door was unlocked," he interrupted.

Savannah ignored him. "Picked the lock on the filing cabinet and was going through my purse."

"Is that right, mister?"

The perpetrator gave a modest little shrug.

One of the security guards took a step toward him, and he raised a warning finger.

"I believe," he said, "your security manual instructs you to wait for the police."

That rankled the guards. "Who the hell are you telling what to do?"

"Maybe you ought to take a second look at who's holding the handcuffs, mister!"

"Not to mention the guns," replied the suspect, "which is something else we'll have to—"

"Hold it, men, he's right!" Savannah had to raise her voice to make herself heard over the din that ensued, and for a moment she thought the two guards would rush him. She wasn't sure whose safety she was most concerned with, that of the guards or their smooth-talking prisoner. "The situation is under control, and your orders are to wait for the police."

The two guards reluctantly acknowledged her authority, although Savannah noticed they seemed to be holding their guns at an even more menacing angle, and they did not back off. Savannah only hoped the object of their surveillance would give them no reason to exercise their very limited and well-defined rights of restraint.

Apparently, the thief was no more anxious to get bloodstains on her carpet than Savannah, for he did nothing but cock his head toward the faint sound of sirens coming from the window and comment, "And here they come now. There, you see, gentlemen, there was absolutely no reason at all for the theatrics. As a matter of fact—"

"What's all the bloody commotion? This had better be damn good, Monterey! Do you know what time it is? Do you know what happened to the last person who woke me at three o'clock in the morning?"

Savannah winced, not from the content of the words but from the sheer volume. The voice, which boomed through the corridors and was fully capable of waking anyone unfortunate enough to be sleeping on the bottom three floors, could only belong to one man.

Greg Walker was just under six feet tall and just over three hundred pounds; he was as formidable in person as his voice implied. Someone had once remarked upon his resemblance to Henry VIII which had resulted, for better or worse, in Greg's growing a beard to match the part. He stood at the threshold of Savannah's office wearing a voluminous white shirt with unbuttoned French cuffs over dark suit pants and a scowl that would have made a linebacker think twice. Utter silence seized the room.

And then the burglar said politely, "Good morning, Mr. Walker. I'm sorry for the disturbance, but it couldn't be helped."

Walker's thunderous expression faded into something closely resembling astonishment as he turned his gaze on the intruder. "You," he said, and his voice picked up amusement mixed with admiration as he added, "By God, you did it, didn't you?"

"I did," he agreed, and then cast a wry glance at Savannah. "Although not entirely successfully, I have to admit. Your assistant manager was a bit more alert than I had anticipated. However..." He started to reach into his pocket, then addressed the two guardsmen with an upraised eyebrow. "With your permission, gentlemen?"

Greg Walker made a brusque gesture with his wrist. "For heaven's sake, put those guns away. This is not a bloody western, you know."

Looking very reluctant indeed, the guards did as they were ordered, though both of them kept a wary eye on their former prisoner as he reached inside his jacket and withdrew a slim manila envelope.

"Yours, I believe," he said, passing the envelope to Walker.

Greg Walker looked into the envelope and then back at the thief. His expression was a mixture of amazement and outrage as he removed a watch. "That's my Rolex! And my ring! And..."

Dark anger suffused his face and then drained, leaving it a somewhat sickly green as he fingered the remaining contents of the envelope. "These papers were in my wall safe. There were negotiable bonds in there...."

"Still there," he assured him. "As are the computer security codes and your personal banking information. I used a passkey," he added. "I could have just as easily changed the key codes through the computer but decided that wouldn't prove anything we don't already know."

He reached into his pocket again and withdrew several more envelopes, passing them out one by one. "The contents of the hotel safe. Deposit boxes 133, 441 and 816. The contents of the cash drawer. Please count it."

Greg Walker looked like a man who was being repeatedly punched in the stomach, and each envelope he accepted was a new blow. Savannah knew how he felt. Her head was reeling and she had to hold on to the desk to support her weak knees. She opened her mouth to demand an explanation but only a croak came out. And then a new voice was added to the din of her thoughts.

"We got a call there was trouble here."

Two uniformed policemen and a detective stood at the door. Savannah recognized Detective Jenkins, who had been working with them on the burglaries. She opened her mouth to answer but once again couldn't make a sound.

It was probably just as well, because he seemed to answer his own question. His eyes fell on the handsome thief and immediately registered recognition. He said in a voice tinged with disgust, "You. I might have known."

The other man returned a smile and another modest lift of his shoulders.

At last Savannah found her voice. "You!" she burst out, rounding on him. "Don't you have a name? Who are you?"

He just grinned, infuriating Savannah.

She turned to Greg Walker. "What's going on here? Who *is* this person?"

It was with obvious difficulty that Walker dragged his attention away from the envelopes that were in his hand, and the battle between shock and admiration was clearly visible on his face. Finally, he seemed to reach some kind of equanimity with the situation, however, and he replied, more or less evenly, "Relax,

Ms. Monterey. This is C. J. Cassidy, our new security consultant."

"Also," added Detective Jenkins dryly, "one of the most notorious burglars on the East Coast."

Two

"So," added Detective Jenkins casually, "how've you been, C.J.?"

"Staying out of trouble, Don. How about you?"

"Doing my best."

"I resent your restricting my fame to the East Coast, by the way. Last I heard, I was the most notorious burglar in the *country*."

"Well, times are changing, my friend. You've got to work twice as hard just to keep up these days."

Savannah felt as though she had stepped through the Looking Glass. "Excuse me?" she croaked. Then, more firmly, "*Excuse* me!"

Both men turned to look at her. Walker, who was busily counting the cash in the envelopes, spared her only a brief annoyed frown.

Savannah demanded, ''Since I seem to be the only one who *doesn't* know what's going on here, would someone mind explaining it to me? After all, the man was apprehended in *my* office, trying to steal *my* purse, and I'd like to know if this...this...burglar is going to jail.''

A look passed between Walker, Cassidy and Jenkins. Walker turned back to counting his money. Jenkins shrugged. It was Cassidy who, turning on another one of those simmering smiles, explained, ''I apologize if you were upset, Ms. Monterey, but I really didn't expect anyone to be here this time of night. I was hired to run a security check on the building, and the best way to do that is from the point of view of a burglar.''

With a heavy sigh, Walker looked up from the envelopes. ''Well, it's all here. The penthouse, guest rooms, cashier's desk, safe. You didn't miss a trick, did you?''

''Well, just one,'' the detective observed. He thrust his hands into his pockets and rocked back on his heels, clearly enjoying the situation. ''The getaway.''

''Ah,'' Cassidy countered with an uplifted finger, ''but I would have managed that, too, if I hadn't stopped to steal a kiss.''

Both men stared at Savannah, and she felt a dull hot prickling in her cheeks, the hollow thudding of her heart. She tasted again the press of warmth against her lips, the hint of wintergreen. She felt the tingling of her flesh, the tightening of her stomach. Then Cassidy directed their gazes pointedly to the chocolate kiss on Savannah's desk.

Savannah felt an absurd surge of gratitude toward him, followed immediately by resentment. Who did he think he was, anyway? How dare he?

Detective Jenkins chuckled as he turned toward the door. "Brought down by a woman, I always knew it would happen. Come on, boys, let's write this one up. Keep in touch, C.J."

"Count on it," replied Cassidy, but his eyes, gently dancing with his own secret amusement, were on Savannah.

Greg Walker said to the guards, "That's it for you, too, gentlemen. If you'll excuse us . . ."

"Just a moment, if you don't mind, Mr. Walker."

Cassidy walked over to the guards, who still regarded him with thinly disguised belligerence. Savannah couldn't blame them. Ten minutes ago, this man had been their prisoner, and now he was acting like their boss—which, if Greg Walker could be believed at this hour of the morning, Savannah supposed he was.

"Would one of you happen to be the night-shift supervisor?" Cassidy asked.

The two men exchanged a look, as though debating whether or not to answer.

"That would be Art Cannon," one of them said finally. "He's manning the desk."

Cassidy's eyebrows drew together sharply. "You get an emergency call from the assistant manager in the middle of the night and the supervisor doesn't even respond?"

"That's the way we're organized around here—"

"It looks to me as though a little reorganization is in order. Please tell Mr. Cannon I'll meet with all three shift supervisors at ten o'clock in the morning to discuss just that. That will be all for now."

The two men looked at Walker as though for confirmation, and the hotel manager gave an almost imperceptible nod. One of them muttered, "Yes, sir," and the two of them left.

The expression on Greg Walker's face was somewhere between admiration and sourness as he said, "I can't say I like your style, Mr. Cassidy, but I must admit you know your business. You've got the job."

Cassidy nodded, unsurprised. He had already arranged to reorganize the security department at ten o'clock in the morning, hadn't he?

Savannah lifted both hands in a gesture of supplication and forebearance. "Now wait a minute. Just wait a minute."

She spoke very carefully, making a valiant attempt to be rational when rationality seemed to have flown out the window. But it was, after all, three o'clock in the morning. Maybe she had missed something.

She said, "Let me get this straight. Is this man a burglar or a security expert?"

Cassidy just smiled. "The fact of the matter is, burglars *are* the top security experts."

He had the single most entrancing smile Savannah had ever seen in her life. He smiled, and she thought of moonlight dancing on water. He smiled, and her skin tingled, her pulse quickened just a fraction, every sense seemed more alert. He smiled and he could have made an astronaut believe the world is flat.

For her own protection Savannah tore her gaze away from that smile. "You're hiring a *criminal* to overhaul our security system?" she demanded quietly of her boss.

For a moment, Walker looked uncomfortable. "As I understand it, Mr. Cassidy has long since given up the, er, questionable aspects of his career. He's a legitimate businessman and comes highly recommended by some of the biggest police departments in the country. He's been on talk shows, for heaven's sake." Greg Walker's manner was growing more irritable by the moment. "You don't think I would have asked him to come here without thoroughly checking his credentials, do you?"

Savannah drew a breath. "Mr. Walker, you know I don't usually second-guess you—"

"And very wise of you, my dear." With those dismissive words, he turned to Cassidy. "Stop by my office in the morning at your convenience. The contract will be ready for your signature, on the terms we discussed. And now, if you have no further surprises planned for the evening, I believe I'll try to catch up on my sleep.''

At the door he glanced back and added, ''By the way, from now on, you will be reporting to Ms. Monterey. She has been working most closely with the security staff on these break-ins and can bring you up to date on what we have so far. Good night.''

And before Savannah could do any more than gape at him wordlessly, he closed the door behind him.

C. J. Cassidy settled on the corner of Savannah's desk, swinging one leg casually, and regarded her with frank and friendly appreciation. ''So,'' he observed, ''the fringe benefits begin already.''

Savannah Monterey had not risen to the position of assistant manager of one of the most exclusive resort hotels in the country at age twenty-six by demonstrating a lack of resolve—or by whining about things over which she had, at the moment at least, no control. She was competent, decisive and capable. She had climbed the ladder of success by working hard and knowing how to take charge. Her superior had put her in charge of this man—this project, she mentally corrected herself—and though it was a situation she had every intention of making as temporary as possible, there was nothing she could do at this hour of the morning except make the best of it.

She returned coolly, ''I wouldn't be counting my fringe benefits, or anything else just yet if I were you, Mr. Cassidy. In the first place, I have quite enough to do without your adolescent cops-and-robbers games. In the second place, if it were up to me, you never would have been hired in the first place, so take my advice and don't get too comfortable in your new position."

He inquired, "Do you always work this late?"

Savannah couldn't help being a little annoyed that her speech had seemed to have virtually no effect. She frowned. "What?"

"For my security files," he explained. "If I'm going to design an effective security program, I need to know who is supposed to be where at what time. Ideally, this entire wing should be shut down and put on an automatic monitoring system at night, not to be disturbed until the next morning."

"That's completely impossible. I need access to my office whenever—" But then she caught herself and broke off. She was talking to him as though it mattered, as though he actually had authority to his situation, as though they were working together.

Briefly she pressed her fingertips to her temples and drew a breath for composure. "Look," she said, "it's three-thirty in the morning. While I realize in your line of work—" she placed skeptical emphasis on the phrase "—you're probably used to these hours, I'm not. What do you say we continue this discussion at a more civilized time of day?"

"Actually," he said, "I've always found the *unciv*ilized hours to hold the most promise."

He slid down off the desk with supple, catlike grace, his voice low and musical, his eyes alight with that subtle polished-stone gleam. His was the kind of sex appeal that could not be learned or imitated; it was inherent, genetic, woven into the essence of his being. It was no doubt his most powerful weapon, first line of defense in his life of crime, particularly when his victims were women.

But Savannah was more experienced than most in that kind of warfare, and she had developed a considerable arsenal of her own. She was five-four, one hundred six pounds. She had long, smooth, baby-fine hair that was bleached by the sun into gradations of every conceivable shade of blond. Her skin was practically flawless; her eyes were emerald green. When she walked into a room, heads turned, and every man there—women, too—saw only one thing: a living, breathing China doll.

Savannah liked to think she was much more than that.

She had been fending off advances from teachers, her father's friends and her sister's dates since she was thirteen. She had long since mastered the art of putting-in-his-place employers and would-be employers, best friends' husbands, potential boyfriends, ex-boyfriends and never-would-be boyfriends. She would have no problem handling one C. J. Cassidy.

All she had to do was ignore those muscular looking legs, refuse to be caught by that smoky gaze, turn away from that full, sensuous mouth...and stop wondering whether or not he had a fondness for wintergreen breath mints.

She kept her manner cool and her voice deliberate as she said, "Before you leave, perhaps you would explain to me just what has been going on here tonight. Or, more precisely, how it is you can just sail in here, steal everything that isn't bolted down, and instead of going to jail, you get a job."

He smiled. "That *is* my job. Mr. Walker hired me to penetrate the hotel's vulnerable areas, then design a system to protect them. Of course, I told him what I was going to do, but not when I was going to do it. That wouldn't have been fair."

"Then I didn't misunderstand. You *are* a professional burglar."

"Was," he corrected. "An important distinction."

He was standing very close, so close that she could smell his scent, and again there was nothing artificial about it. It was innate and masculine, faintly reminiscent of the night breeze that swept over the sea, salty fresh and clean and uniquely his own. Savannah ignored it as best she could and looked deliberately into those silver eyes.

"So you're reformed. And I'm supposed to trust you."

He tilted his head a little, a gesture that was almost as endearing as his smile. "Well, now, I wouldn't say that exactly. In some situations a little healthy mistrust can be a very exciting thing."

Falling for his charm, Savannah could tell immediately, would be a great deal easier than resisting it. Deliberately ignoring the slight increase in the pace of her pulse, she informed him, "I want you to know I don't believe a word of it. I don't trust you out of my sight—or in it, for that matter—and first thing in the morning, I'm going to do everything I can to sever whatever dubious connection you might have with this hotel."

"Pity," he said, though he did not look in the least distressed. "I was so hoping we could be friends."

Savannah frowned sharply. "You play dangerous games, Mr. Cassidy. What if I'd had a gun instead of an umbrella stand?"

He countered quietly, "What if I had?"

He reached out then and grasped a strand of her hair, and Savannah wasn't certain whether the sudden chill that tingled along the course of her spine was caused by his words or in simple response to his touch. Then he smiled, and tucked the strand of hair behind her ear. "Be more careful, will you, angel? I have a feeling I'm going to have enough on my hands without worrying about you."

Savannah swallowed hard. Surely he hadn't really moved closer; it must only seem that way to her harried imagination. But was that the faintest hint of wintergreen on his breath?

She said steadily, "Good night, Mr. Cassidy."

He smiled. "Do you live in the hotel?"

He was definitely standing too close, but Savannah refused to be the one to move away. This was, after all, her office. She was in charge.

"Do you need to know *that* for your security files, too?"

The smile deepened at one corner, igniting a gentle spark in the depth of his eyes. "No," he responded. "The information is for my personal files. I'm in suite 300, by the way."

Savannah squared her shoulders and tightened her lips against the effects of his insidious charm. "I wouldn't unpack if I were you."

He laughed softly. "I was right. I *am* going to have my hands full."

He stepped past her toward the door, then turned back casually. He held her watch between his fingers. "By the way, might I also suggest that you guard your personal belongings more carefully?"

He released the watch to her indignant grasp and winked at her. "Who knows? Next time I might try to steal more than a kiss."

Pausing only to scoop up the morsel of foil-wrapped chocolate from her desk, he sauntered out of the room.

Savannah did not, in fact, live in the hotel—that was a privilege reserved exclusively for the manager, who held the ultimate responsibility for the smooth operation of the hotel, was on call for all emergencies and, in theory at least, worked far longer hours than Savannah did. But in the past two weeks, she had learned the wisdom of keeping an overnight bag at work so that, on nights when she worked past midnight, she could slip into an empty room and get a few hours' sleep before starting another day.

The Boheme was one of the most exclusive resort hotels on the East Coast. With its twin grand staircases, light-filled atrium and shell-pink carpeting, it recalled the grandeur and luxury of a bygone era. Discretely elegant shops were tucked into nooks and crannies along the way, marble vases filled with thousands of dollars worth of fresh flowers were liberally placed on every available surface. But the star attraction was a three-story aviary in the center of the lobby, complete with a waterfall and living tropical plants, graced by over a dozen species of brilliantly colored birds. Savannah never walked through that lobby without feeling a surge of wonder and pride that she was a part of all this.

Located on Sandstone Island off the southern Florida shore, it had played host to kings, presidents and heads of state in its long and colorful history. For Savannah, the assistant manager position at a hotel like The Boheme was a dream come true.

For the south Florida beach hotels, the busiest season began in January and lasted through March. Though The Boheme did not really have a slow season, the first week in January heralded the onslaught of the year's wealthiest and highest-paying guests, many of whom made The Boheme a tradition year after year. That was why the rash of burglaries that had afflicted the hotel since Christmas was so disturbing. And that was why, no doubt, Greg Walker had been moved to such desperate measures as to hire a man like C. J. Cassidy to solve the problem before it got even more out of hand.

Savannah arrived at her office the next morning feeling grumpy, disheveled and bleary-eyed. It had been almost five o'clock before she got to sleep, and then her dreams had been troubled by laughing gray eyes and full sensuous lips. Naturally she had overslept and that irritated her, because she had planned to beard Greg Walker in his den first thing that morning and demand he see reason. Furthermore, the only outfit that had come back from the cleaners in time for her to toss into her overnight bag was one of her least favorite—a linen suit consisting of sand-colored city shorts, a long, full-cut jacket and a peach silk blouse. It wasn't that she didn't think the outfit was attractive; she simply found it completely inappropriate for the office.

Her only hope of salvaging the morning was if her boss was getting a late start, as well, and she managed to catch him *before* Mr. C. J. Cassidy oiled his way even further into the manager's confidence. Such was not to be her luck.

Her secretary, Holly, met her with a handful of message slips and a look of flushed excitement on her face that Savannah knew instinctively could only have been put there by one man.

"Have you met him?" she demanded breathlessly. "The new security chief?"

Savannah scowled as she took the messages into her office. "Consultant," she corrected shortly. "He's only a consultant, and his job is very temporary."

Savannah did not have an ocean view—such amenities were reserved for paying guests—but she did have a window with an impressive view of a megaton air-conditioning unit and the tops of several dark green dumpsters. Every morning, Holly, in addition to starting the coffee in Savannah's three-cup brewer, made sure to open the blinds to the view. And every morning, Savannah, after pouring her first cup of coffee, closed them.

She set the messages on her desk and went to pour the coffee.

"Oh." Holly sounded disappointed, then brightened philosophically. "Well, all the more reason to enjoy the scenery while he's here. Don't you think he's just gorgeous? I mean, doesn't he remind you of an American James Bond?"

Savannah closed the blinds. "James Bond is a fictional character."

"I know that," responded Holly, affronted. "Anyway, he was here earlier. And he wanted to know if you were free for lunch. I penciled him in for one."

Savannah sorted the message slips into three piles: urgent, important and someone else's problem. "Well, you can just erase him. Get me Housekeeping on the phone, please, and ask Mr. Walker when it would be convenient for me to see him.''

Holly seemed to take particular pleasure in replying, ''He's in with Mr. Cassidy, and they ordered breakfast, so it will probably be a while. I'll get Housekeeping for you. And don't forget the staff meeting at eleven.''

''Great,'' Savannah muttered as Holly closed the door quietly but firmly behind her. She *had* forgotten. The staff meeting was in fifteen minutes and it would take her that long to return the calls in her ''urgent'' pile. And why should she feel miffed that Greg Walker had *not* invited her to his breakfast with C. J. Cassidy?

But, perhaps most frustrating of all, she could not even look around her own office without seeing reminders of his invasion of the night before. The cocky grin, the smoky eyes, the long, slender fingers . . . the taste of wintergreen. And being reminded was like a series of soft, tingling and not altogether unpleasant electric shocks.

The housekeeping supervisor had a list of complaints that ranged from being shorted on their sheet delivery to the draperies that had been tied in knots by the occupants of room 817. Every problem had to be taken seriously and dealt with promptly, as Housekeeping, next to Dining Room, was the very lifeblood by which a hotel survived. She had barely hung up the phone when Holly rang to say Stan Keller, the chief of security, was on the other line. Savannah was not surprised. Three of the "urgent" messages were from him.

"Look, Ms. Monterey, we've got to talk about this so-called security consultant of yours." Stan had never been one to mince words, and these words were not only to the point, they were spoken at something very close to full volume. "Do you know what he did last night? Do you?"

"He broke into the safe, the penthouse, the cash drawer and several guest rooms," she said.

Stan paused for only a beat of surprise. "And this is supposed to prove something? This is supposed to impress us? Let me tell you about these hotshots with their bagful of tricks, and I've seen plenty of them, believe me—"

"I understand perfectly, Stan—"

"Now don't you start with that 'I understand' talk, or your fancy security consultant can just consult with somebody besides me. I don't trust him, Ms. Monterey, and you don't have to be a security expert to come to *that* conclusion."

"You're right," Savannah replied. "I came to the same conclusion last night right after I found him going through my purse."

This time, the pause was more significant. "Well," he said gruffly. "Well there, you see what I mean. Now, I'm warning you, this man is trouble, and if you expect me to sit back and take orders from him, you might just be in for a big surprise."

Savannah's second line was blinking. "I'm on my way to talk to Mr. Walker about that very subject. Let me see what I can do and get back to you, may I?"

It was with a kind of grim satisfaction that she disconnected the call. At least she wouldn't be the *only* person on staff with objections to the illustrious Mr. Cassidy, and it couldn't hurt to have the head of security on her side.

But her sense of triumph faded as she pushed the button on her phone and was plunged into the next urgent call. It was from the kitchen manager, who had been at knifepoint with the new chef—figuratively if not literally—for the past six weeks.

"The man is impossible!" raged Mac Rinshaw. "Forty minutes before the dining room opens, Armand informs me he can't make the quiche without imported black olives! The quiche *he* put on the menu! The quiche that should have been in the *oven* by now! I'm telling you Ms. Monterey, I don't know how much longer I can put up with this. Half the waiters are ready to quit—"

"I know, Mac," soothed Savannah, "but all the great chefs are said to be temperamental...."

She had more to say but suddenly lost her train of thought as she glanced up and saw C. J. Cassidy lounging in the doorway.

He was wearing khaki pants and a pale blue shirt unbuttoned at the throat. His thick dark hair, casually brushed away from his forehead, gleamed with bluish highlights, his eyes smiled lazily. At this hour of the morning, there was only the faintest trace of beard-shadow on his lower jaw, but Savannah could see at the open throat of his shirt a hint of the silky black mat of hair beneath. She swallowed hard and tried to remember how long it had been since she'd been with a man with hair on his chest.

"The man thinks he's the last great hope of the American people!" Mac was fuming, and Savannah dragged her attention back to him reluctantly. "Well, I'm here to tell you The Boheme was getting five-star ratings long before he came along and will continue to get them long after he's gone! As far as I'm concerned—"

"I'll talk to him," promised Savannah. "You just relax and leave it to me."

She hung up the phone without being entirely sure the other man had said goodbye.

"Good morning, angel," said C. J. Cassidy. He looked infuriatingly well rested, not to mention well fed. Savannah was starving.

She gathered up her notebook and began the search for a pen. "I'm sorry, Mr. Cassidy, I don't have time to talk to you now. I'm on my way to a meeting." And with any luck, she added silently, by the time I get back, you will no longer be employed here.

She slid open a drawer, but found no pen.

Cassidy said, "I know. I stopped by to escort you."

She stared at him. "*You're* going?"

"Greg thought it would be a good idea if I met the department heads this way first, and sitting in on a meeting will give me a feel for the way the hotel operates.''

So much for her plans to have a few words in private with Mr. Walker about the latest addition to their payroll. And he called him *Greg*, Savannah couldn't help but notice resentfully.

She slammed the drawer shut and opened another. ''I don't need an escort.''

''But maybe I do. The new guy in town and all that.''

She slammed shut another drawer. ''It doesn't look to me as though you're having any trouble at all making friends. You had breakfast with the boss, didn't you?''

He clicked his tongue against his teeth in gentle reproval. ''Jealous, Ms. Monterey? I wouldn't have thought it of you.''

Savannah gave up on her search for a pen and stood up. She would borrow one from Holly. ''Believe me, Mr. Cassidy, if I were going to be jealous, it certainly wouldn't be of a common criminal.''

''I beg your pardon.'' His eyes were amused. ''I have been called many things, but *never* common.''

He stepped forward, and before she could guess what he was going to do, he lifted his arm and plucked a pen from behind her ear. He smiled. ''Is this what you were looking for?''

Savannah kept her voice mild despite the racing of her heart—from surprise, nothing more. ''Why is it that every time you show up, things start to disappear?''

He grinned. "Coincidence, I'm sure."

She snatched the pen from him and started toward the door.

"You're not going to leave your purse?"

She shot him a sharp look. "It's in a safe place."

"The file cabinet?"

Her frown deepened. "It's locked."

A raised eyebrow explicitly demonstrated what he thought of *that* precaution, and Savannah knew he was right—as he had so deftly proven last night. Irritation tingled in her cheeks, but she ignored it.

"You're welcome to anything I have in my purse, Mr. Cassidy," she said breezily, brushing past him. "Now, if you'll excuse me."

He kept step with her, and Savannah was acutely aware of Holly's bright-eyed gaze following them across the room. In the hall, he inquired, "Why do you disapprove of me so much?"

She gave a short bark of laughter. "Isn't that obvious?"

"Maybe *disapprove* is the wrong word. Maybe..." His tone was thoughtful. "Afraid?"

She paused in stride long enough to toss him a sharp incredulous look. "Don't be absurd!"

But the thoughtful, faintly amused look on his face didn't fade. "Yes," he murmured. "I'll have to give that some thought."

Outside the door to the conference room, Savannah turned to him. "Mr. Cassidy," she said with as much patience as she could muster. "You'll find that most people who earn their money the old-fashioned way are just a little resentful of people who steal for a living. A quirk, perhaps, but one you'll just have to get used to."

"Ms. Monterey," he replied, matching the forced politeness in her tone, "I am going to tell you this one more time—I don't steal for a living, I keep other people from doing it. I'm on your side now—difficult for you to grasp, I know, but you'll just have to get used to it."

He opened the door to the conference room and with a small, mocking bow gestured her to precede him.

Three

This really is an impossible situation, Savannah reflected more than once during the meeting. The heads of every department in the hotel were present—security, maintenance, housekeeping, food services, engineering, front desk, guest services—but Savannah was only aware of Cassidy. He sat across from her, his long legs stretched beneath the table, idly turning a silver pen over and over between his fingers. Every time Savannah glanced up, he was looking at her with that same speculative amused look in his sultry gray eyes. He was doing it just to torment her, Savannah knew. She never should have said what she had about the way he made his living. It was a cheap shot and unworthy of her.

But she was partly responsible for this hotel and what went on within it. It was her job to be concerned about everyone who walked through that door, whether guest or employee. With a resumé like his, Savannah would not have hired C. J. Cassidy to wait tables, much less supervise the security staff.

Besides, he made her nervous.

"—as I'm sure Ms. Monterey would agree."

The voice belonged to Greg Walker, and Savannah jumped at the sound of her name. She realised that the last time she had been listening, the discussion had centered on whether or not to switch linen suppliers. She didn't know the outcome of that question and heaven only knew what she was supposed to be agreeing to now. Damn Cassidy, anyway. This was her *job,* the most important thing in the world to her; Cassidy had been here less than twelve hours and already he was interfering with her ability to do it.

She very wisely made no reply to Walker's assumptions, ignoring the twinkle in C. J. Cassidy's eyes, and pretending to busy herself with making a note on her pad.

"Now, on to our most important piece of business. As you're all aware, the house is ninety percent sold for the month of January. As you're also aware, we've been experiencing an unsettling number of break-ins and petty thefts over the past few weeks, and that's something we have no intention of tolerating. It's taken three-quarters of a century for The Boheme to build the kind of reputation that attracts some of the most discriminating guests in the world, and we certainly can't afford to jeopardize it now.''

Greg Walker tended to become a bit impassioned in defense of his hotel, and he harrumphed angrily before continuing. ''Toward that end, I'd like to introduce to you C. J. Cassidy, a private security consultant who will be working with us to update the hotel security system. Mr. Cassidy.''

Cassidy's smile went round the table, easy and casual. His position was relaxed, with one arm outstretched on the table, shoulders slouched back against the chair; even his slightly tousled hair seemed designed to inspire an at-ease atmosphere. And, as though his smile were a magic wand, everyone he smiled at seemed to be instantly charmed—with the exception of Stan, the security chief. Again, Savannah mentally fortified herself with the knowledge that she had at least one supporter in the campaign against C. J. Cassidy.

''I look forward to meeting with each of you personally,'' Cassidy said. ''It's impossible for me, as an outsider, to come into your hotel and solve your security problems. I need input from the real experts— you.''

Bingo, Savannah thought, and she couldn't help but admire his style. He couldn't have found a faster way to win their trust if someone had drawn him a blueprint.

''Naturally, I'll want to ask a few questions about how your departments run—to find out what your needs are, and to make sure I don't get in the way while I'm trying to design a program that will make everyone happy."

Again, he favored them with one of those heart-melting smiles, and Savannah's admiration became mitigated with irritation. He was a little *too* good at this.

"I'll also want to meet some of your key people and get your ideas on where you think the biggest security risks are. The kind of episodes you've been having here aren't unusual for a hotel this size. Our goal is not to just stop these burglaries, but to look to the future, and put a program in place that will prevent anything like it from happening again."

Savannah was almost moved to applaud. She had an unpleasant suspicion, in fact, that the entire room might have burst into a round of welcoming applause and had he not added, "I'll be making appointments with each of you starting today, but if there are any questions now, I'll be glad to answer them."

Lisa Mare, housekeeping supervisor, raised a timid hand. C.J. smiled at her and Savannah half expected the older woman to melt into a puddle right before her eyes. She said, "You're not going to make the women take lie detector tests, are you? Because they all had background checks before they were hired, and half of them have threatened to quit if they have to take a lie detector test."

"In a situation like this," Cassidy replied seriously, "I've found lie detectors can do more harm

than good. And I believe your own security chief—"
he gave a salutatory nod in Stan's direction "—has all
but eliminated the possibility that the thefts are inside
jobs. So, no, I won't be putting any hotel employee
through the inconvenience of a lie detector."

Stan looked somewhat mollified, Lisa looked practically radiant, Greg Walker looked smug. Savannah
thought sourly, *I'd like to see you pass a lie detector
test, Cassidy. On this or any other subject.*

Walker waited a polite moment before bringing the
meeting to a close. "I'm sure you will all give Mr.
Cassidy your fullest support and cooperation over the
coming weeks. And in the meantime, just to keep life
interesting, I hear through the corporate grapevine
that we can expect secret shoppers some time during
the next month."

The groans almost drowned out his next words.
"Secret shopper" was the code phrase for the undercover inspectors the hotel chain sent out from time to
time to rate the house and expose weaknesses. They
couldn't have chosen a less propitious time.

"So let's look sharp, ladies and gentlemen. Until the
same time next week . . ."

He rose, signaling the meeting was adjourned. Savannah, sitting on his left, spoke quickly before anyone else could demand his attention. "Mr. Walker,
could I have a few minutes?"

"Of course, my dear. I'm on my way to the gym.
Walk with me."

Greg Walker liked to do his part for physical fitness by putting on a sweat suit and a pair of two-hundred-dollar shoes and taking a stroll around the indoor track at least once a week. Savannah, like everyone else on staff, was fond of her boss and liked to encourage any effort he made toward better health, but on this occasion, she wished for a more private meeting.

Almost as though lying in wait to sabotage her plans, C. J. Cassidy lingered as everyone else left, holding the door for her. "We're on for lunch, Ms. Monterey?"

"I'm afraid not." Savannah walked briskly through the door, not glancing at him. "I'm busy for lunch. My secretary will reschedule." *Never, with luck,* she thought, lengthening her stride to keep up with Mr. Walker.

She had hoped Cassidy would take the hint, but people with his kind of ineffable self-confidence rarely responded to subtleties. "Dinner, then?" he called after her.

And before she could reply, Greg Walker answered, "Fine, good idea, she's never busy for dinner. Make it early, though. I don't like my employees keeping late hours, it cuts down on efficiency."

Savannah was so flabbergasted she couldn't speak. She actually stood still in her tracks, staring at Mr. Walker's back as he continued forward and stabbed the elevator button. She turned back to Cassidy in frustration but caught only a glimpse of him, leaning against the doorjamb of the conference room and grinning, before the elevator doors slid open. She had to run to catch up and squeezed in beside her boss.

There were two guests on the elevator. Savannah smiled at them and then looked straight ahead until they exited at the next floor. When they were gone, she said, "I think that was out of line, sir."

He shot her a quick astonished frown. "What?"

"Your telling Mr. Cassidy I'm available for dinner and making a date for me! You made it sound as though I don't have any social life at all."

He made a brusque dismissive gesture. "Who cares about your social life? This is hotel business."

"Maybe I didn't want to have dinner with him."

"Why in the world shouldn't you want to have dinner with him? He's a perfectly presentable young man, clean and well groomed. I had breakfast with him only this morning and can tell you his table manners are quite acceptable." He spared her a narrow look. "And since when did you let what you want interfere with the performance of your duties? Is there something going on between you and Cassidy that I should know about?"

"Of course not!" Savannah couldn't keep the exasperation out of her voice—or the faint flush off her cheeks. "That's precisely my point."

But when he simply continued to study her with that partly puzzled, partly suspicious look on his face, she gave up and closed the subject with a helpless shake of her head. "Just don't make any more dinner dates for me, okay?"

He replied stuffily, "I wasn't aware that I had."

The elevator bell chimed and the doors slid open. They stepped off.

"It was Mr. Cassidy I wanted to talk to you about, as a matter of fact," Savannah said.

"I thought you just had."

His dry humor was sometimes hard to take.

They turned down the rose-carpeted corridor that led to the eight-floor gym and sauna, and Savannah knew her time was limited. She took a deep breath and plunged ahead.

"Mr. Walker, I know you assigned me to work with Mr. Cassidy, but I'm not sure that's possible. The fact is, I have my doubts about his integrity, and frankly, so does Stan."

"Come, come, Ms. Monterey, that demonstration last night was precisely that—a demonstration, and I should think you would be as impressed as I was."

"Of his skill at breaking and entering? Absolutely! And that's only one example—"

"Ms. Monterey, please. Let's not belabor the obvious. Aside from last night's little performance, what can the man possibly have done in such a short time to make you question his integrity?"

Savannah pressed her lips together briefly. If several thousand dollars in jewelry and cash could not make Mr. Walker see her point, what difference would the report of a stolen kiss make? If indeed, he had stolen it.

"Mr. Walker," she began again firmly, "you have to admit the man's background leaves a great deal of room for suspicion. Maybe he has built something of a reputation in the security business, but this isn't an ordinary hotel, and I can't help worrying about our guests. Why, Emily Bouvier alone could keep the ordinary thief busy for weeks just picking her pockets, and you're suggesting we open up our entire security system to a man who used to do just that for a living? I'm just not comfortable with that, sir. Not at all."

"You're quite right to be concerned about the guests, of course," replied Walker soothingly. Because he was never soothing, Savannah was immediately alerted.

"Now, I'm sure you would never doubt *my* integrity," he went on, "or question *my* judgment. And I have made the decision, haven't I, Ms. Monterey?"

Savannah stiffened her shoulders. "Yes, sir."

They had reached the glass doors of the gym. Walker paused there with his hand on the handle, looking down at her. His smile was kind, with just the right touch of royal condescension. "You are an excellent second-in-command, Ms. Monterey, which is a simple necessity when one runs the kind of tight ship I do. You've brought your concerns to my attention, which is no less than duty demands. Is there anything else?"

Savannah knew she had to play every card, and this might be her last chance. "Mr. Walker, Stan has been head of security here for three years. Aside from the fact that it will be almost impossible to do an accurate security audit without his cooperation, I think we owe it to him to at least listen to his opinion about Mr. Cassidy. If we can't respect his judgment in a matter like this, what have we been paying him for all these years?"

Walker nodded thoughtfully. "Quite right, of course. Your challenge then, is to get Stan's complete cooperation and assure him that we do respect his judgment while, in fact, proceeding with our own agenda. I'm sure you're more than worthy of the task, my dear. Anything else?"

Savannah drew in a sharp breath through her nostrils, but she knew better than to argue. With defeat looming before her, she was nonetheless compelled to add, "Just one more thing."

He looked at her questioningly.

"You put him in one of our best suites."

He lifted an eyebrow. "Yes?"

Her jaw tightened briefly. "That suite was sold for practically the entire season. We're looking at a substantial loss of revenue here. Surely other arrangements..."

"I'm afraid not. The suite was part of his contract. Now, is there anything else?"

Savannah swallowed hard. She had given it her best shot. "No, sir."

He looked at her meaningfully. "You're sure?"

Savannah knew this was her last chance to object, to refuse to work with Cassidy or to make it clear she was incapable of working with him. She also knew she would not do anything of the kind, and so did Greg Walker.

She said, "I'm sure."

He nodded, and pushed open the door of the gym. "Very well, then, Ms. Monterey, I leave the matter in your hands. And I rely upon you to do your usual excellent job."

Savannah smiled feebly, even though Walker could no longer see her do so. "Yes, sir."

And, having no other options, Savannah turned back toward her office to begin doing her job.

Four

C. J. Cassidy could not afford many weaknesses, and the only one he allowed himself—the only one, in fact, that he couldn't seem to rise above—was his love of beautiful things. It was this passion that had, throughout his life, toppled his better judgment, persuaded him to take absurd risks and had been known to cause him more trouble in a single day than the average man faced in a lifetime. His fascination with beauty and the constant temptation it presented was a dangerous diversion, but one he found almost impossible to resist.

Savannah Monterey was one of the most beautiful things he had seen in a long time. Certainly she was the most dangerous.

At precisely six o'clock that evening, he tapped lightly on her office door and stuck his head inside without waiting for a reply. She was busily stuffing papers into a briefcase, trying, he suspected, to escape the office without meeting him. He repressed a smile.

"Caught you," he said.

She frowned without looking up. "I don't know what you're talking about."

"You were trying to duck out on our date. Dinner, remember?"

The frown deepened. "Don't be ridiculous, of course I remember. And it's not a date."

The tight bun into which she had wound her hair was not quite as neat as it had been this morning, and most of her makeup had faded. The linen suit was a little rumpled, and the bow tie on her blouse hung limply at her throat. Cassidy thought she looked at least as alluring now, at the end of a hard day's work, as she had when he had first come upon her last night, sleeping like an angel.

He came into the room. "You're a bad liar. I like that."

"I hope you won't mind if I don't spend a lot of time debating the merits of honesty with you."

She put just enough emphasis on the last word to make sure he knew it was an insult. Cassidy was not insulted.

"Not at all. I can think of better ways to spend the time."

Savannah closed her briefcase, buckled it neatly and looked up at him. "I have you on my calendar, Mr. Cassidy—dinner tonight. You're welcome to see for yourself. I didn't forget, I had no intention of avoiding you. I very often have to work through dinner, it comes with the job."

"Well, well. I misjudged you. My apologies."

"Accepted. Did you reserve a table downstairs?"

"No. What changed your mind?"

The frown touched her forehead again, but it didn't last long. She glanced at her watch. "It's early. Jackson probably has a table, but he'll be mad if we don't let him know we're coming. I'll just call down."

She reached for the telephone, but he lifted a staying hand. "No need. I've made other arrangements."

Suspicion darkened her eyes from aqua to emerald. It was an enthralling process to watch. Cassidy wondered what hues her eyes might take on in the throes of deep anger... or pleasure.

She said, "I really don't have time to leave the hotel."

"We won't go far," he assured her.

Savannah replaced the receiver and picked up her briefcase. The expression on her face was polite, regretful and well rehearsed, but beneath it was a hint of unmistakable relief. "Mr. Cassidy, I've been working overtime for the past three weeks and I really am exhausted. I haven't even been home for two nights now. I've had a really hard day and I'm just not up to a formal dinner out, so why don't we do this another time?''

He chuckled. ''There's nothing formal about it, don't worry.'' He extended his hand. ''Come on, you have to eat, and I promise you'll be home in two hours max.''

When she still hesitated, he added, ''You know you're going to have to do this sooner or later. May as well get it over with.''

''I suppose so,'' she agreed unhappily. She stood. ''But I'm driving my own car.''

''Again, not necessary. It's within walking distance.''

Her forehead furrowed thoughtfully. ''But there's nothing . . .''

''You didn't answer my question,'' he interrupted, touching her back lightly as she came around the desk. He could feel her react, ever so slightly, to his touch, though she pretended not to.

''What question?''

''What changed your mind?''

She shrugged. ''Greg Walker runs a tight ship and I'm a good little soldier—or sailor, as the case might be. I might not always agree with his decisions, but I do know who's boss and who's just training to be boss. So I try not to waste too much energy beating my head against brick walls.''

''Very practical of you.''

Walking half a step behind her, he couldn't help admiring the way the long lines of the jacket flattered the flare of her hips, and the way the shorts cuffed just an inch or two above her slender knees. He wondered if she was wearing any stockings. He couldn't imagine a woman as precise as she was coming to work without them, but her legs were so smooth and evenly tanned it was hard to tell.

In the outer office, he stopped to sweep a picnic basket off the receptionist's desk. It was wicker, tastefully stamped with the hotel logo and packed with cold chicken, crab cakes, a very nice champagne and a host of other delectables. She stared at it.

"You got Armand to make you a basket? He hates doing that! He doesn't even do it for paying customers without putting up a fuss."

He held open the outer door for her. "People tend to like me, which means they do things for me. Charm is a necessary skill in my line of work—or I should say *former* line of work."

"I will have to remember that," she murmured dryly.

Though the look she slanted him was skeptical, she did walk through the door, which, until that moment, he hadn't been entirely sure she would do.

"I certainly hope you're not planning to charm me with a picnic on the beach," she added. "Been there, done it and I'm not impressed."

"Thanks for the warning. I try not to waste my charm on people who don't appreciate it."

"With so much of it to waste, I should think that would be the least of your concerns."

He grinned. "And I was afraid you wouldn't like me."

"I'm not at all sure I can afford to like you, Mr. Cassidy. Not until I know what you expect me to do for you, anyway."

"What makes you think the pleasure of your company isn't enough?"

Again she shot him a dry look. "I thought you weren't going to waste it."

He shrugged. "I prefer to think of this as an investment."

"Until you decide what you want from me?"

"Good shot," he murmured, and his admiration was genuine.

"Besides," she went on, "if I thought the pleasure of my company—or any other kind of pleasure—was all you were interested in, I wouldn't be having dinner with you and certainly not a picnic dinner on the beach. I give you more credit than that."

For the first time in many years, Cassidy felt he was on the verge of being in over his head. It was intoxicating.

"I appreciate that," he answered cautiously. "But may I ask why?"

"Anyone who's smart enough to con Greg Walker, as well as Detective Jenkins, is not going to blow it with a lowly assistant manager. Particularly when that assistant manager has already made it clear she doesn't trust him...and is waiting for him to make a mistake. No, with me you're going to be extra-careful, extra-professional and—'' she glanced up at him again ''—unless I miss my guess, extra-charming.''

He gave a small shake of his head. ''Damn. I hate being predictable.''

He had the satisfaction of seeing the corners of her lips tighten with a smile and was surprised to realize exactly how much satisfaction that gave him. He was accustomed to women smiling at him; how odd that a smile from this woman should seem so precious. Perhaps it was because the smile had been so hard to come by.

They exited the hotel via the courtyard, a nostalgic old-world garden that was choked with bougainvillea, draped with wisteria and studded with little stone benches built for two. The courtyard opened onto a sand-drenched wooden walkway that led directly to the beach, and he gestured her toward that path.

Cassidy inhaled the evening air deeply. ''This is the life, isn't it? I can't think of anything that smells better than sea air.''

''I can. Lots of things. Almost anything that doesn't use dead fish as a base.''

She stopped and slipped off her sandals as they reached the top of the steps that led down to the sand. No stockings, Cassidy noticed. He smiled.

''Ever-practical, I see,'' he said. ''Most people think the ocean is romantic.''

''Which is exactly why resort hotels are built on beaches and employ people like me,'' she replied flippantly.

The wind caught her hair from the front and the sides, whipping loose several strands, which she pushed back impatiently. Cassidy wondered how long it would be before the wind defeated the very businesslike chignon entirely, and he wondered why a woman as practical and unromantic as she professed to be would choose to keep her hair so long.

He said, "You really are lucky, you know. Working in a place people pay hundreds of dollars a day just to visit, all this for your front yard..." He made a sweeping gesture toward the indigo ocean and twilight, the nearly deserted beach. "Not to mention temperatures of eighty-six in January. I'll bet you don't have much to put on your wish list these days."

She shrugged, stepping down into the sand. "It's just a job."

He stared at her. "A job? You're living in paradise and you call it a job? There are only a couple of hundred thousand people—myself included—who would love to have your job."

She glanced at him with puzzled amusement, as though trying to determine whether or not he was serious. "I think you mean that."

"You better believe it. As a matter of fact, I think I might just put your job on my five-year plan right now."

Savannah chuckled. She couldn't help it; the thought of a man like C. J. Cassidy with a five-year plan was more than a little funny. And it was amazing, how easy it was to laugh around him, how natural it felt to relax and enjoy his company. But what was it he had said? Charm was an essential skill in his line of work?

She said, "Of course, for the next few weeks—or months, as the case may be—you don't have to envy my job. You have one that's even better."

"Or it would be, if it weren't temporary."

Again Savannah slid a quick glance at him, disguising her puzzlement beneath lowered lashes. He sounded so much like any other man, with perfectly ordinary hopes and plans and dreams, that for a moment even she was convinced. He was good. Damn good.

She said, "Where are you from?"

"Denver. It gets cold in Denver."

She walked along the cool sand. The last light of day left the sky a pale washed-out blue, and the shadows were long and purple across the sand. Sea grass rustled and snapped with the wind, and the surf sighed and breathed and sighed again. Savannah thought it was probably all rather romantic, if one noticed that sort of thing... and if one were with the right man. Savannah made it a point not to look at the man she was with right then.

"That wouldn't have been my first choice," she said.

"What, Denver?"

"Somehow, you don't tend to think of professional criminals coming from some place like Denver.

Detroit, Chicago, New York—one of those would have been my guess.''

"Well, now, that's what makes this country great, isn't it? Even a boy from Denver can grow up to be a jewel thief.''

Savannah was intrigued despite herself. "Is that what you steal—stole? Jewels?''

"Among other things. Paintings, objets d'art, Egyptian artifacts, Faberge eggs . . .''

Until that point, he'd had her enthralled; then, her lips tightened with disgust at her own gullibility and he flashed her a quick grin.

"All right,'' he admitted, "no Faberge eggs. No Egyptian artifacts, either, though I spent most of my career looking for a chance to get my hands on both. How about over there?''

He gestured to a spot in the shelter of a tall dune where high tide had packed the sand down flat and smooth. Savannah followed him.

"Quite a few objets d'art, though,'' he went on easily, "and more paintings than you might expect.''

"Do you mean,'' she ventured hesitantly, and wasn't sure she wanted him to answer, or that she should believe him if he did, "like Rembrandt and Renoir and—''

He interrupted her with a dismissive grunt of laughter. "I should be so lucky.'' He set the basket on the sand and took a plaid blanket from inside. "If I could have put my hands on a Rembrandt just once, I assure you I wouldn't be standing here with you now, talking about my illustrious career in the past tense.''

That shouldn't have surprised Savannah but somehow it did. Surprised, intrigued and confused her.

She caught the ends of the blanket as the wind billowed it upward, and helped him to spread it on the ground. ''You make it sound glamorous.''

He shrugged. ''I don't mean to.''

She studied him with interest in the dying light. ''But it was.''

His smile was slow and easy and left far more hidden than it revealed. ''I thought we were going to talk business.''

She countered, ''I thought that was what we were doing.''

The smile turned rueful, though there was a spark of admiration far back in the depth of his eyes that he couldn't hide and didn't try to. ''You're not going to make this easy, are you?''

She dropped to her knees on the blanket, brushing out a few wrinkles. ''Easy is boring,'' she replied. She settled down and arranged her legs in a very proper and ladylike fashion to the side of her.

Cassidy studied the arrangement of her legs with appreciation, then knelt beside the picnic basket and began to unpack it. ''I don't imagine very many men are bored around you.''

''I don't know that anyone has ever taken a survey, but I do know one thing.'' She smiled sweetly. ''As long as you're in my hotel, I will make it my personal mission to make sure there's never a dull moment in *your* life. Consider yourself forewarned.''

He murmured, ''I don't suppose there's any point in hoping you meant that in anything other than a professional way?''

''I mean it,'' she replied evenly, ''in the same way any assistant manager would talk to a security expert who used to be a thief . . . a thief specializing in hotels, I might add.''

He removed a towel-wrapped bottle of champagne from the basket and turned it expertly between the palms of his hands. ''You've done your homework.''

''Part of the job.''

The champagne cork gave a muted pop, and a fine froth spilled over onto the towel. Cassidy took a glass from the basket and filled it, his eyes holding hers with speculative interest. ''Why do I think you're starting to enjoy that part of the job more than others?''

Savannah pushed a strand of hair back behind her ear. It was a self-conscious gesture she usually tried to avoid, but tonight she had the wind to blame. ''I don't know what you mean.''

He handed her the glass of champagne. His thoughtful, faintly amused look did not fade. It was unnerving. ''I mean I think I'm starting to understand something very interesting about you. I think you find hotel thieves much more exciting than hotel detectives—or security consultants, as it happens. And I think you're having a little trouble admitting that to yourself.''

"I think," Savannah answered without blinking, "we should talk about how you expect to do an effective job as a security consultant when the man you're supposed to be consulting with wants to have you arrested."

He filled his own glass. "Stan Keller doesn't like me because I pointed out that in the two and a half minutes it took his team to get to your office last night, you could have been dead, raped or set up in a hostage situation. I also pointed out that the way his men barged in there like cowboys in an old Western could have resulted in a lot of blood on the floor if I had been desperate and armed."

His tone was matter-of-fact, holding the easy competence of a seasoned professional. He went on, "You get a lot of wealthy, influential guests at The Boheme Hotel, many of them politicians and celebrities—the kind of guests whose presence invites terrorists and assassins. Seventeen percent of them do *not* travel with their own security teams. Frankly, the situation at The Boheme is a disaster waiting to happen and I'm surprised you've avoided it this long."

Savannah stared at him, a little disoriented. One moment he was a charming thief, the next a perfectly competent policeman, and it was hard to tell which was his true persona. Worse, Savannah did not know which one she preferred.

She said, a little dazed, "Terrorists, assassins... I thought all you were supposed to do was investigate a few burglaries."

He said, still with that same air of casual competence, "I'm being paid a lot of money for this job and there's no point in doing it halfway." He tasted the champagne, nodded appreciatively to himself and set the glass aside as he began to unpack the basket. "It wouldn't do my reputation much good if, a month after I approved your security system, someone like the Pope was kidnapped while staying here, would it? A thing like that could put me out of business."

Savannah sipped her champagne. "Fortunately, you have other skills to fall back on."

His eyes sparked quick amusement—along with a measure of exasperation—as he glanced at her. "Fortunately."

Savannah tasted the champagne again and held up her glass in approval. "Nice champagne. Armand must really like you. I don't suppose you could speak to him about being more cooperative with the kitchen staff, could you?"

"I'll see what I can do. Now, isn't this better than eating in a crowded dining room?"

Savannah filled her plate with chilled shrimp, chicken, cheese and fruit. She had to admit, if only to herself, that it was wonderful. Cassidy had even thought of candles—the oil-based kind, protected by wire baskets, that would keep their flames in the wind. He lit two of them as the last of twilight gave way to purple evening, and their swaying, flickering light kept rhythm with the crash and whisper of the surf.

Champagne, candlelight and a man like C. J. Cassidy sitting across from her, one arm propped on his upraised knee, his dark hair tousled by the wind, looking exotic and mysterious and even a little dangerous, his profile turned toward the sea...it was hard to think of this as a business meeting. It was hard not to see the entire setting as just a little bit romantic. And it was far too easy to relax and start to enjoy it all. She hadn't had an evening off in far too long.

Deliberately, she focused on the task at hand. This was not, she had to remind herself, an evening off.

"I assume you read my report on the state of the investigation so far," she said.

He turned his head to look at her, and the slow curve of his smile suggested he knew exactly how difficult it had been for her to remain businesslike. "I have," he said.

He tore off a bit of chicken with his fingers and popped it into his mouth. The gesture struck Savannah as a little pagan, oddly sensual, and she wondered if he had intended it to be. On the other hand, he could probably make a cheese sandwich seem erotic. Sexuality, in all of its subtle and varied forms, was never far from the surface with him, Savannah realized suddenly. Whether he intended it or not, whether she consciously recognized it or not, that singular masculine allure was always there, pulsing just below the surface like a low electric charge, reminding her with every look, every gesture and every word of the difference between men and women.

"—until I finish interviewing everyone on staff," Cassidy was saying. "That shouldn't take more than a few days."

Savannah realized to her chagrin she hadn't the faintest idea what he was talking about. She disguised the fact with a smile and a nod, and bit into a wedge of apple.

"I expect your burglary problems are over, at least for a while. And by the time the season gears up, the new security system should be in place, so we might just squeak by on this one."

"What makes you think the burglaries are over?" As easy as it was to be distracted by the way the candlelight etched shadows on his face and played across the open neck of his shirt, that statement was too sweeping to ignore.

"The thief knows I'm here. He'd be a fool to try anything now."

Savannah chuckled. "So the mere rumor of your presence is enough to send potential thieves running for cover. Maybe we should have saved ourselves some money and simply bought a cardboard cutout of your likeness to stand in the lobby."

"It's been known to work," he agreed modestly, and leaned forward to refill her champagne glass.

She held up a hand in protest. "No, please. One more glass and I'll be asleep before I get home."

"I'll drive you."

Savannah smiled. "No," she said. "You won't."

"Of course." He refilled her glass, anyway. "That would make this seem like a date. Or maybe you just have a policy against going out with people who have criminal records."

She looked at him curiously. "You really don't mind, do you?"

"Mind what?"

"Talking about your past, having other people talk about it."

"Actually," he answered, refilling his own glass. "I mind very much. But it doesn't really matter. People are going to talk about it, and if I don't, they'll think I have something to hide. Which of course I do."

She smiled and sipped her wine. "You are a very intriguing man."

The wind whipped across the dunes, making the candles shudder and snatching several long locks of Savannah's hair from the pins that confined them. She tried to recapture them but it was a losing battle. Finally, with a little laugh of surrender, she simply pulled out the comb that held her chignon in place and shook her hair loose around her shoulders.

Cassidy caught his breath. Once, in Belgium, a flawless blue diamond had caught his eye. He'd seen it lying there against a background of black velvet, and the sensation that had gripped him was so visceral, so singular and paralyzing that it transcended mere desire. He'd looked at it, and he knew he had to have it.

He looked at Savannah now, with the wind whipping her long golden hair, and the candlelight glowing and flickering on her face, he heard the soft husky sound of her laughter, saw the sparks in her eyes and it was Belgium all over again. He knew he was lost.

The diamond had turned out to be a fake and the man who owned it an undercover cop, and one might have thought Cassidy would have learned his lesson by now. One would have been wrong. Back then, he would have moved heaven and earth to make that stone his, and today he would do the same for the woman who sat across from him, all cool skepticism and snappy comebacks, the angel in the business suit with a laugh that went straight through his heart.

Another gust of wind chased her hair, and before he could stop himself, his hand reached out to capture a lock. She looked surprised, but the smile in her eyes did not fade, it merely transformed into something more uncertain, aware and expectant, as she watched him. He wound the strand gently around his fist, leaning closer, and closer, until their faces were within touching distance. Easily.

She didn't pull away, or even try. Her voice sounded just a little breathless as she said, "I thought we were going to keep this on a professional level."

He answered softly, "I told you, I hate to be predictable."

Her hair felt like silk around his fingers, and her perfume, a subtly exotic blend of tropical flowers and sea breezes, seemed to drench his pores. By a fraction of an inch, he leaned closer. Her eyes, her skin, her face filled his vision. And still, she did not move away.

She said, in a voice that was almost steady, "You're taking a big risk, you know."

"Life's a risk." His lips were almost brushing hers. He could practically taste her. "That's what makes it interesting. Why don't you trust me, angel?"

Savannah drew in a short breath and his scent seemed to fill her—champagne, herbal soap and warm, strong masculinity. She could feel every cell and pore open to him, anticipating him, and the sensation made her skin ache.

She swallowed hard, but no power on earth could have compelled her to move away from him. And her voice still sounded hoarse. "Do you mean besides the obvious?"

His eyes moved over her face and her throat, seeming to caress each place they examined. The sensation of being touched was so strong, Savannah actually arched her neck a fraction, appreciating it.

He said, "There's nothing obvious about it to me."

His voice was low and husky, and his fingers, the ones that were still wound about the lock of her hair, brushed her jaw. The skin prickled at the base of her spine and spread slowly downward to her toes.

Somehow, she focused her concentration. She even managed to make her voice sound calm and detached. "I think you went a little beyond the call of duty last night when you broke into my office."

The back of his knuckle stroked her jaw, just beneath the earlobe. The sensation was exquisite.

She took a steadying breath. "I dreamed someone kissed me. I woke up and you were there."

The faintest trace of a smile curved his lips. Lips that she remembered so well—or had imagined so completely. Lips that even now were only a breath away from tasting hers, from proving what was real and what had been dreamed.

He suggested, "Kismet?"

His knuckles traced her jawline forward to her chin, and his fingertip etched a shallow semicircle at the corner of her lips. Savannah could not reply.

"Now, angel, that would be a foolish thing to do." His voice was soft, bordering on a seductive whisper. His eyes caught the candlelight with an almost mesmeric glow. "Why would I risk my job, my reputation and a harassment suit for the sake of one kiss?"

She kept her gaze steady, although all she really wanted to do was lean back, close her eyes and let the night happen. "I don't know. Why would you?"

Again the faintest, most entrancing hint of a smile. "You may never know."

A breath, a sigh, the merest puff of wind would bring them together, mouths seeking and exploring, soft breasts pressed into hard chest muscles, arms entwining. All she had to do was close her eyes, sink into him, let it happen.

He whispered, "Aren't you even curious?"

His eyes filled the night, his lips brushed hers when he spoke and sent little rivulets of pleasured anticipation through her veins. A flick of her tongue and she would be tasting him, a softening of muscles and she would be in his arms.

She said, "No." Her voice was hoarse, perhaps because her heart was pounding in her throat. "That's another luxury I don't think I can afford. And neither can you."

Then, with more willpower than she thought she possessed, she turned her head and calmly took a sip of champagne. Or at least she pretended calm. Actually, her hand was shaking and quite a bit of the champagne splashed onto her fingers, but in the dark she hoped he wouldn't notice.

She could feel his gaze on her for another long, resolve-weakening moment. And then, slowly, he unwound the lock of hair from his fingers, letting it fall in a single long curl across her left breast. He stroked the curl lightly, lingeringly, and Savannah's heartbeat stopped in expectation of his touch. His fingers barely brushed the material of her jacket over her breast. It was sublime torment. He moved away.

After a moment, Savannah risked a glance at him. The thoughtful, slightly introspective look on his face prompted her to ask, "What? What are you thinking about?"

He gave a wry shake of his head, glancing down into his glass. "Belgium," he said. "A certain blue diamond, a certain undercover policeman."

She relaxed a little and her heartbeat began to resume its normal rhythm and she moved on to more comfortable ground with him. "Is that how you got caught?" she inquired curiously.

His reply was flippant. "I never got caught." He drained his champagne and started repacking the basket.

She leaned forward to help. "Put out of business, then." Her curiosity deepened. "What did happen? The reports weren't clear on that and your resumé certainly didn't say."

The tightening of the lines on his face was almost imperceptible, and nothing in his tone changed, but to Savannah it was as though a shutter had been slammed shut, sealing him off from her. He replied lightly, "That's right, it didn't."

He finished packing rather quickly, and when he extended his hand to help her up, Savannah said, somewhat uncertainly, "Well, thanks for dinner. It was nice. Although I can't help but feel we didn't get much accomplished in the way of business."

"More than you know," he replied cheerfully.

"Like what?"

"I eliminated you as a suspect for one thing."

And, while she simply stared at him speechlessly, he picked up the blanket, shook out the sand with one snap and draped it over his arm.

"Ready to go?" He walked her to her car, and by that time was surveying the parking lot with the practiced eye of a professional. "There are a few dark spots here," he commented. "I'm going to have to recommend more lighting."

"This is a luxury hotel, not an airstrip," Savannah responded irritably. She inserted her key into the lock.

Cassidy leaned against her door, his smile slow and seductive and seeming to hide a secret knowledge of every thought that had ever gone on in her head. He said, "You're not sorry, already, are you?"

Savannah twisted the key curtly. "About what?"

"Not finding out."

She gave him the coolest stare of which she was capable—which was considerably cool. "Good night, Mr. Cassidy. Thank you again for dinner."

He reached into his pocket and brought out a roll of candy. "Mint?" he offered.

She looked at him. She looked at the candy. She couldn't help herself. She took one.

His eyes were twinkling as he moved away from the door. "Good night, angel," he said.

Savannah got inside the car and was preparing to slam the door when he said, "Just one more thing."

When she looked up, he was leaning over the open door, a pair of earrings dangling from his fingers. Immediately, her hand flew to her ears. The gold hoops she had placed there that morning were no longer there. They were, in fact, in C. J. Cassidy's hand.

He dropped the earrings into her lap. "Pleasure doing business with you, Ms. Monterey. Drive carefully."

She slammed the door, and he got his hand out of the way just in time. She could feel him grinning after her as she drove out of the parking lot at a faster-than-recommended safe speed.

By the time she reached the exit to the main road however, she was calm enough to remember the candy in her hand. Curiously, she popped it into her mouth.

It was wintergreen. Of course.

Five

Sandstone Island was one of the small barrier islands off the east coast of Florida. Its entire industry consisted of two gas stations, a convenience store, three souvenir stands and The Boheme Hotel. Most of the hotel employees lived in Santee, a midsize village twenty minutes away. Savannah and a few other senior staff members were lucky—or unlucky, depending on how one looked at it—enough to rent one of the small inland houses on the island.

The subdivision in which Savannah's house was located had been part of a developer's ill-conceived scheme to accelerate the growth of the island, but the plan had failed before it reached fruition. On the positive side, the houses were widely spaced and well screened by the heavy foliage of the lots that had never been cleared, giving it more of an atmosphere of a jungle plantation than a subdivision. On the negative side, the streets had never been paved, the plumbing was erratic and in the rainy season, Savannah's entire handkerchief-size front lawn turned into a marsh.

However, this was not the rainy season, Savannah had not had any trouble with her plumbing in almost a month, and she was celebrating the first day off she had had in three weeks by sleeping late. Except for the faraway chime of a bell that kept trying to rouse her from her blissful half-dreaming state, Savannah hadn't a complaint in the world.

In her waking life Savannah was practical and efficient, but in her dreaming life she was extravagant. Today she dreamed of a jungle ripe with lush white flowers and black-green foliage, and a waterfall pool as blue as a surrealist painting. A black-and-orange jungle cat walked beside her, and as she parted the leaves to peer into the waterfall pool, she saw a figure swimming there, just beneath the surface. It was sleek and naked and male, and just as it was about to rise up out of the water, the faraway ringing started to intrude, nudging her out of sleep.

Drowsily disappointed, Savannah let the remnants of the dream drift away as she stretched and turned over in bed. She could feel the sun on her face from the three uncurtained windows that surrounded her bed, a gentle warmth that was filtered through the thick foliage outside into lacy shadows and soft colors. Flinging back the pastel sheets, she stretched again, then drew up her knees and burrowed her face more comfortably into the pillow, preparing to take the waking-up process in a leisurely fashion. She opened her eyes a slit, then a little more.

A sleek male figure was standing beside her bed.

Her eyes traveled over a pair of legs neatly encased in sand-colored cotton, over thighs nicely accented by a multitude of fashionable and well-placed pockets, moving upward to a slim waist and the perfectly proportioned flare of a masculine chest, then onward to the strong lines of a tanned throat and the dark shape of his jaw. By the time her eyes reached his face, Savannah was feeling no surprise whatsoever.

She demanded in a flat tone, and with very little animosity, "What are you doing here?"

"I rang the bell," Cassidy answered by way of explanation. "I assumed you didn't hear it."

"Most people," Savannah stated, without moving so much as an eyelash, "would have assumed I wasn't home. Or that I wasn't answering the door. Most people might have even gone away."

"Well," he admitted modestly, "I always have had an overly developed sense of responsibility, and I didn't feel right about just walking away without checking out the situation."

"How did you get in here?"

"Breaking and entering does happen to be my specialty," he reminded her.

She mumbled, "Of course," and closed her eyes again, perhaps with some vague notion about pretending the entire episode had been a dream.

She tried to conjure up some outrage, she really did. But at this hour of the morning, such emotions were entirely out of her range. And to be perfectly fair, C. J. Cassidy's presence in the hotel was largely responsible for the way things had calmed down over the past week, which was the only reason she had been able to take a day off. In a nicely convoluted way, one could even say that he was the reason she had been sleeping late in the first place, and if he chose to disturb that sleep, it might even be called his right.

Besides, she had awakened to more unpleasant sights in her day.

She was half tempted to just let herself drift off, and she might have done so had she not become increasingly aware of his gaze. Her eyes were closed and she had no way of knowing whether he was looking at her or not, yet her skin tingled. And she knew without opening her eyes exactly where his gaze would be resting.

She was lying on her stomach, hugging the pillow with both arms. One knee was drawn up higher than the other, causing her nightshirt to ride up high on her thigh, close to the panty line. She felt the caress of Cassidy's gaze there, sweeping down the curve of her bare leg.

He moved his eyes deliberately away from that enticing view and scanned his surroundings. Savannah's bedroom was painted pale yellow. Her sheets were goldenrod and even her nightshirt was a floral print on a pale yellow background. When she opened her eyes to the haze of morning sunlight filtering through, it was like being bathed in a golden glow. Or perhaps that feeling was generated solely by the look in Cassidy's eyes as his gaze moved from her naked leg to her face.

That look alone made her heart seem to swell in her chest, and she thought how easy it could be for him to sit beside her, to let his fingertips replace his stroking gaze, tracing the shape of ankle and calf, delving into the sensitive flesh behind her knee, caressing the shape of her thigh and creeping upward. Would she stop him? She didn't know, and that disturbed her.

Would he sit down beside her? Would he rest his hand on her leg, would he begin to bring her fantasy to life? For a moment, she almost thought he would.

Then he smiled, and his voice sounded a little husky as he murmured, ''Maybe I'd better make some coffee.''

There was a faint film of perspiration on Savannah's upper lip when he had gone. She told herself it was only from lying in the sun.

She took her time showering, and changed into a pair of shorts and an oversize cotton shirt tied low on her hips. She braided her hair into a long loose rope that hung down the middle of her back. She was aware that she was stalling, half hoping he would get tired of waiting for her . . . and half hoping he wouldn't.

It was her day off, after all, and he had some nerve disturbing her at home—not to mention breaking into her house and waking her from a sound sleep. She had every right to be annoyed with him and no obligation whatsoever to be polite.

Nonetheless, there was a little tingle of excitement in her stomach as she left the bedroom, following the scent of freshly brewed coffee to the kitchen—and a definite surge of disappointment when she found the room empty. She poured herself a cup of coffee, trying not to feel too foolish for the flutter of anticipation she had allowed herself to enjoy, and noticed the clock read ten-thirty. It was high time she was up, anyway.

And then she saw him, lounging in one of the patio chairs just outside the sliding glass doors. Savannah couldn't help it; she smiled.

The most charming feature of the house was a tiny courtyard, accented by a flagstone patio just large enough to hold a glass-topped table and two wrought-iron chairs. The courtyard was completely surrounded by shrubs and trees, and wherever there was a blank space or an inch of ground, Savannah had placed a flower bed, or stacked planters filled with cascading ferns. The effect was lush and verdant, and it pleased Savannah in a purely inexplicable way, that he had discovered her favorite spot so quickly and seemed to be enjoying it so completely.

She stood at the door for a moment, watching him. His legs were outstretched, his elbows resting on the arms of the chair as he sipped coffee from a rainbow-colored mug. His head was tilted back to catch the broken patches of sunlight, and his face was relaxed and content. For a moment, she was puzzled by his expression, wondering why it seemed so familiar to her, and then she realized it was the same expression she wore on her own face whenever she sat in that garden.

The recognition left her with a sense of closeness to him, of surprised understanding. This exotic creature who brought danger and unpredictability everywhere he went, who could heat her blood with a look, was nonetheless completely at home in her garden. He was ever a mystery, and that only made him more exciting.

She slid open the door and stepped out. He said, without turning his head to look at her, "This is spectacular. Why would you ever want to go to work and leave it?"

Then he glanced at her as he sipped his coffee. "Of course, my personal taste runs to turn-down service and ocean views, but I can see why you might like it."

Savannah sat down in the other chair. The table was so small that when she put her coffee cup down at the same time he did, their hands brushed. She thought, but couldn't be sure, that he might even have prolonged the contact a second or two. Or perhaps it was simply her imagination that suggested this.

She said, "Where do you live?"

"A hotel."

"No, I mean when you're not working."

"A hotel. I have a suite at the Miami Regent."

Her reaction was somewhere between a puzzled frown and an admiring laugh. "Are you serious? And you like it?"

He shrugged. "Completely maintenance-free living. It's close to work, never needs cleaning and room service is only a phone call away."

She nodded, picking up her coffee cup. "I used to think I might like living in a hotel—at some places that's an option with a managerial position. But room service and clean sheets wouldn't make up for phone calls in the middle of the night..." And she glanced at him wryly. "Like the one Mr. Walker got the first night you came on duty."

He affected innocence, and she sipped her coffee. "Besides, the truth is, in this business you move around so much you learn to make as much of a home for yourself as you can while you can. That's why I like gardening." She made a small deprecating gesture toward the courtyard. "It makes it all seem permanent, even if it's not."

She glanced at him, a little self-conscious for having spoken so freely. Over the past week, he had been in and out of her office, they had consulted briefly, passed in the hall, spoken for a few minutes at a time. Nothing of a personal nature had passed between them since that night on the beach, and it had not been her intention to open the door to personal confidences now.

But to her surprise, he was nodding. "I know what you mean. Maybe I should take up gardening. Of course, in my case, it would have to be a dish garden."

She said, "I don't understand. You can live anywhere you want. You just told me you like living in a hotel."

"It's not the same as a home, though, is it?" He drained the last of his coffee. "They say you can't miss what you've never had, but I could argue with that theory. More coffee?"

"Help yourself," she murmured.

He flashed her a grin as he rose. "I always do."

Interesting man, she thought, and followed him into the kitchen.

"What did you come out here for, anyway?" she asked, a little ashamed that she hadn't thought to ask before.

"What kind of question is that to ask someone who was just about to offer to make you breakfast?"

When he held up the coffeepot, she let him refill her cup. "The kind asked by someone who hasn't had a day off in three weeks. Do you have an answer?"

"Not one that you'd like. I came on business." He opened the refrigerator door and peered inside. "Those papers on the table need your signature."

She glanced at the manila folder on the table, then at him. "What are they for? And what are you looking for?"

"Eggs, milk, butter..." He straightened up, his arms filled with the aforementioned items. "I make a hell of an orange French toast. You do have bread, I presume?"

"Oatmeal-bran. And how could you possibly know how to make French toast—or anything else—when you just told me you'd never had a home of your own?" She moved forward to take the ingredients to the kitchen table.

He grimaced. "Oatmeal-bran. That's the best you can do?" He retrieved the carton of eggs from her. "All right, French bread would be better, but I'll take what you've got."

Savannah opened her mouth to protest again, but let it close on silence. How often, after all, did she have a chance to have breakfast prepared for her by a professional thief? She turned to get the bread.

"I need your signature to authorize the new key-card system I'm installing," he said. He opened a cabinet and, on the first try, found a mixing bowl.

Savannah put the bread on the counter beside him. "We just installed a new key-card system two years ago!"

"So I noticed. Unfortunately, it's more of a security risk than a security device. On average, it takes a guest three tries to get his door open, and while he's standing out in the hall, juggling luggage or packages or beach bags and swearing at the key card, anything could happen. Pickpockets and muggers—not to mention other, even less savory sorts—would call a situation like that a bonanza.''

She watched him crack eggs into the bright blue bowl with all the easy efficiency of a Parisian chef, and it was difficult not to be impressed. Impressed, she clarified to herself admiring and just a little flattered . . . all those emotions men spent an inordinate amount of time trying to elicit from a woman when all they had to do, really, was make themselves at home in her kitchen. Was there anything sexier than a man with his sleeves rolled up and his hair tumbling down on his forehead, flour on his hands and a mixing bowl resting in the crook of one arm? Or maybe, she had to correct herself honestly, it was just *this* man, who could look sexy reading a comic book.

She forced her attention away from his physique— and the easy, confident moves that complemented it— and on to the matter at hand. With pretend casualness she flipped open the file that held the papers.

''My signature couldn't have waited until morning? You had to disturb me on my day off?''

''Considering the fact that I ordered the system a week ago—no, it couldn't wait. Butter?''

''Margarine.'' She went to the refrigerator to get it for him.

''And your complaints are starting to sound a little insincere. After all, you're getting a gourmet breakfast out of it.''

"Breakfast, maybe." She eyed the concoction in the blue bowl doubtfully. "Gourmet...we'll see. Shouldn't you add salt?"

He lifted an eyebrow meaningfully. "You know what they say about too many cooks..."

She took her coffee to the breakfast bar and settled down to watch him work. Her gaze must have been more intent than she realized, because after a moment he seemed to become aware of it. He glanced at her with an odd little smile.

"You're different here, aren't you?"

She sipped her coffee. "What do you mean?"

"Not so uptight. Calmer, more relaxed." And he looked her over thoughtfully. "Younger."

She laughed. "I'm not sure that's a compliment."

"Just an observation."

He began to rummage through the cabinets and this time she did not offer to help. Eventually, he came up with the proper size skillet on his own. Savannah watched him set the margarine on to melt with one hand while whipping the batter to a froth with the other. She had to admit he knew his way around a kitchen.

"Where *did* you learn to cook, anyway?" she inquired curiously.

"I spent the best part of my life in the world's finest hotels, remember? Where there are fine hotels, there is usually fine dining."

"Ah." Savannah nodded sagely, regarding him over the rim of her cup. "So when you finished emptying the hotel safe of cash and jewels, you'd pop by the kitchen and steal Chef Jean-Pierre's recipe for bouillabaisse?''

He grinned, deftly slicing the crusts off the bread. "Something like that. So what's the secret? Why aren't you this much fun at work? I was beginning to think it was something about me that took the sparkle out of your eyes whenever I came into a room."

He was much more likely to put the sparkle *in* her eyes, Savannah thought, as he very well knew. But out loud she merely said, "The workplace isn't supposed to be fun. That's why they call it work."

But the look he gave her compelled her to honesty: she didn't know why. She wasn't even sure what he was doing in her kitchen making her breakfast, but she was certain that was a strong contributing factor to the sense of comfortableness she felt with him.

"It's hard enough for a woman like me to be taken seriously in this business," she said with a shrug, "or any other for that matter. I have to work twice as hard to prove my competence and be twice as strict to get respect. That doesn't leave a whole lot of time left over for fun."

He arranged the slices of French toast into the sizzling skillet, using his fingertips to prod them closer together. Savannah smiled over her coffee cup as she watched him. He said, without turning around, "So you're a victim of your own ambition."

"Aren't you?"

"Another thing we have in common. What are you smiling at?"

At first, she was too startled to respond, wondering if psychic powers were another one of his secrets—or perhaps eyes in the back of his head. Then she saw her face reflected in the shiny surface of the toaster oven and she relaxed.

"I was just wondering what you'd look like wearing an apron."

"And nothing else?" he suggested.

That time, she really was startled into silence—not only because that had been what she was thinking, but because it was the last thing she had expected to hear him say. She wasn't even sure how she felt about hearing him say it. But then, as he moved to turn the toast over in the pan, she caught a glimpse of the twinkle in his eye.

"Well," she conceded, lifting her cup to him, "maybe a pair of cowboy boots."

He laughed. His eyes snapped and his teeth flashed and Savannah thought, not for the first time since opening her eyes that morning, *What an incredibly attractive man!* And not for the first time in his presence, her heart beat a little faster, as she experienced his laughter.

He said, "I do believe I like you better outside the workplace. Come on, grab your plate. A meal like this was meant to be enjoyed alfresco."

They took their plates to the patio table and sat down. Savannah tasted the French toast.

"This is good," she said, trying not to compliment him too extravagantly. But she took another bite and had to add, "This is *really* good."

"Thank you. It's gratifying to know I have an alternate career to fall back on if the security business bottoms out."

The sun had grown high enough to break through the thick shield of foliage that screened Savannah's private courtyard, splattering the patio with lacy shadows and radiant heat. Cassidy's face was planed with gold, his eyes like silver in the moonlight. Savannah was enchanted, and there was no point in trying to deny it, even to herself.

Most people would describe Savannah as leading the perfect life—a glamorous job, living in paradise, youth and independence. In fact, there was very little time left over after work for glamour and Savannah led the most boring life of anyone she knew. Breakfast at home with a handsome young man was not a usual occurrence for her. Breakfast with a handsome young jewel thief was definitely a phenomenon worthy of note.

He said, "If you hate it so much, why do you keep moving around?"

It took her a moment to focus on what he was saying. "I'm sorry. What?"

"A while ago, you were talking about how much you'd like to have a permanent home. So why don't you just stick with one job and stay put?"

She shook her head wryly. "You'd never get anywhere in this business if you did that."

"Where do you want to go?"

"Go?"

"I mean, it looks to me as though you've already gotten somewhere. What more do you want?"

For a moment, Savannah was taken aback. She had never actually sat down and thought about it before. "Well...as far as I can, of course. Manager of one of the American hotels in Europe, or maybe New York. Corporate headquarters someday."

"Corporate headquarters are in Chicago, I believe," he observed. "Windchill gets to forty below there this time of year. I can definitely see why you'd want to give all this up for that."

"Physical comfort isn't everything," she retorted. But she had to admit, when he put it like that, the prospect of achieving her ambitions did not sound all that appealing.

"Anyway," she added, feeling a little defensive, "what about you? Why don't you settle in one place?"

"Who said I wanted to?"

"You did. You said you knew the feeling of not having any place to call home—which I've got to tell you, by the way, I find hard to believe."

"What, that I'd like to have something more in my life than a mailing address? I may be a hardened criminal with horns and a tail but I do have needs, you know."

Though his voice was flip, there was a slight hardening in his eyes, as though to disguise hurt. Savannah was chagrined.

"I didn't mean—"

But he shrugged it off. "Even if I did want something more, it would be pointless. My work takes me all over the world, and a hotel suits me fine." Then he smiled, as though to assure her he had not taken offense and glanced around the garden. "This *is* nice, though."

Then he turned back to his meal. "How did you get into the hotel business?"

"That's a dull story. You don't want to hear that."

"Sure I do."

"I'd rather talk about you."

He gave her a twinkling look. "We know how I got into the business. So tell me about it."

She looked at him curiously. "Why in the world would you want to know?"

He answered, "Because you interest me."

And as closely as she looked, Savannah could not find any sign of deception on his face. She interested him. *She* interested him.

Men did not usually find Savannah interesting. They found her beautiful, sexy, alluring, seductive. They looked at her and they thought of pleasure. They courted her, wooed her, tried to impress her and all the time, their thoughts were on what she could do for them. They never found her interesting, just for herself. She hardly knew how to respond.

Silhouette Reader Service

Freepost

P.O. Box 236
Croydon
Surrey CR9 9EL

Send NO money now

Free Books and Gifts claim

Yes Please send me four FREE Silhouette Desires together with my FREE Gifts. Please also reserve a special Reader Service subscription for me. If I decide to subscribe, each month I shall receive six superb new titles for just £11.40 postage and packing FREE. If I decide not to subscribe I shall write to you within 10 days. The FREE books and Gifts will be mine to keep in any case. I understand that I am under no obligation whatsoever. I may cancel or suspend my subscription at any time simply by writing to you. I am over 18 years of age.

9S4SD

Ms/Mrs/Miss/Mr _____

Address _____

_____

_____ Postcode _____

Signature _____

MAILING PREFERENCE SERVICE

"What was it?" he prompted. "Daddy owned a chain?"

She laughed. "Hardly. Daddy would consider that occupation crass materialism. Both my parents are too busy saving whales and rain forests to sully their hands with building fortunes."

He lifted an eyebrow, recognizing the slight bitterness in her voice she hadn't bothered to hide. "There, you see? I told you you were interesting."

"My parents are interesting," she corrected. "I'm dull and ordinary."

"Radicals, are they?"

"Ex-radicals. Now he's a civil rights attorney and she's an artist—and not a very good one, I'm afraid. I've got one sister in the Peace Corps and another who works for public television, so you see, I'm really the black sheep of the family. Dull, staid and capitalistic to the core."

He nodded. "So that explains it."

"Explains what?"

"Your name. I wondered what kind of people would name their child Savannah."

Savannah gave a grunt of laughter. "That's nothing. My sisters names are Flower and Poppy. I count myself lucky."

He laughed and she cocked her head toward him curiously. "What about C.J.? What does that stand for?"

He replied promptly, "Competent and Judicious."

"Very clever. I told you about my whole family and you won't even tell me your name?"

"Not on the first date," he assured her. "And we haven't even had that yet."

He leaned back in his chair, coffee cup cradled in both hands, his eyes alight with a thoughtful smile. "That must be an incredible feeling—to know where you came from, what you're made of, and even what you're rebelling against."

She spoke without thinking. "You're an orphan?"

"More or less." He sipped his coffee and spoke matter-of-factly. "My mother hung around until I was twelve or so, but she had so many boyfriends in and out, she hardly even noticed I was there. Then one day, she just didn't come home, and I was on my own."

He glanced at her, as though gauging her reaction. Savannah was careful not to show one.

"You surprise me," he commented, finishing off his coffee. "Most women have that social-worker look on their faces by this point in the story. You know, the one that says 'Poor child, no wonder he turned out the way he did.'"

There was such easy amusement in his eyes that Savannah had to wonder whether anything about his story was even true. She answered, "In the first place, no one with any sense would ever feel sorry for you. In the second place, you probably came from a nice middle-class family with every advantage, and you have no one to blame but yourself for the way you turned out."

"You're right about that. None of us have anyone but ourselves to blame." He picked up his plate and hers and started toward the kitchen. "I'll clear the table, you wash your dishes."

She followed him with the coffee cups, but by the time they reached the kitchen, she couldn't control her curiosity any longer. "All right, I've got to know. Was it true or not?"

"My life story? Absolutely true."

"Then I don't understand..." She hesitated, not certain how to put it into words.

"How I rose above my unfortunate beginnings? That was due to Toby."

"Who was he?"

"The man who saved me from a life of street gangs and drugs. He taught me how to recognize a painting by the artist and a jewel by the cut—and he taught me the art of acquiring and disposing of each." He ran water over the dishes in the sink.

"A thief," Savannah said.

"A master thief," he specified, drying his hands. "And whatever else you might think about my basic education, you've got to admit that, if nothing else, Toby taught me to run with a slightly higher-class crowd than I might have done, otherwise."

He turned around, leaning against the sink as he casually rolled down his sleeves. The twist of his lips was a little wry, but the expression in his eyes was alert and watchful. "Not quite the glamorous background you expected, hum? I hope you aren't too disappointed."

The kitchen was small, and the space between the sink and the table even smaller. It was in that space that Savannah stood, and when Cassidy turned around, he seemed to fill the area; there might have been eighteen inches between them but his presence was so quietly commanding, it filled the gap. He was so close, and she was so intensely aware of him that her throat felt tight, and her voice was a little husky as she answered, "It's hard for me to imagine anything about you ever being disappointing, Mr. Cassidy."

The corners of his lips softened, and a seductive gleam appeared in his eyes. "Why, whatever can you mean by that, angel?"

She didn't shy away from the smile that could melt ice. Nor did she flinch from that gaze of his, thoughtful and caressing, that made her skin tingle as it moved slowly from the curve of her collarbone to the tips of her bare toes.

She said, "Just look at yourself. You're flamboyant, exciting, as smooth as silk and a little dangerous. You've led the kind of life people make movies about and you've got enough fast-talking charm to be the envy of any self-respecting politician in the country. Not to mention . . ."

And when she hesitated, he supplied unerringly, "My incredible good looks?"

"Well, yes," she admitted grudgingly. "Sex appeal is always a factor."

"A factor in what?"

He was enjoying this. Savannah was starting to feel a little warm. But she had started this conversation and she wasn't about to back down—or to let him know he had intimidated her.

"A factor in this whole fantasy you create, this James Bond scenario. Glamour, daring, savoir-faire— you've got it all and you put it all together perfectly. You never give anyone a chance to be disappointed. You've got the act down pat."

The smile in his eyes only deepened, and his hand reached out and captured hers by the fingers. He said softly, "And that's what you like about me, isn't it, angel?"

With a gentle pressure, he pulled her closer an inch, then another. Savannah did not resist, though her heart felt like an overweight butterfly in her chest.

"I never said I liked you." A shortness of breath all but robbed the words of their conviction. "Although I find you—interesting."

"Irresistible," he corrected.

Savannah did not know how it had happened but somehow he had pulled her so close their bodies brushed. She could feel the strength of his muscles against her bare thighs, and when he spoke, the words were practically whispered into her mouth. She knew he could feel the pounding of her heart, though her breast barely brushed his chest.

He lifted her hand and, watching her eyes as he did so, turned her wrist to his lips. First the soft and heated pressure of his lips, then the caress of his tongue stroked her pulse point. Savannah felt the sensation all the way to the pit of her stomach, and her knees went weak.

His tongue swept slowly upward over her inner arm, pausing at the crevice of the bend in her elbow, pushing up the baggy shirt sleeve as he moved ever so slowly toward her neck. Rivulets of flame spread through Savannah's veins, constricting her lungs and heating her skin. It was easy, all too easy, to imagine her body spread naked before him while he gave the same attention to each of her limbs....

She whispered, "Well, maybe just a little irresistible."

His fingers threaded through her hair, pressing against her skull, and his lips closed on her neck. Savannah closed her eyes and let herself sag against him, dizzy with the sensation.

He murmured, "I'm going to be the biggest adventure you ever had, angel." And then his mouth covered hers.

Savannah thought, I *know,* and she sank helplessly into him.

Her tongue met his in a slow exotic mating dance, heat and pressure flooding her veins, softening her muscles. Colors swirled behind her closed eyelids and there was a high, sweet ringing sound in her ears. This was no tender, half-imagined kiss stolen from a sleeping woman; this was a slow and thorough invasion of body and soul and Savannah felt it right down to the tips of her toes.

The taste of him filled her, his very breath expanded her lungs. His muscles were hard and sleek against her hands and the heat of his body flowed into hers, setting her skin on fire. Her muscles turned to clay, ready to be molded by his expert touch, and her will evaporated beneath the magnetic power of his.

His mouth moved to her face, her neck, the closed crescents of her eyes. His thumbs massaged the sensitive hollows at the base of her ears while his fingers spread through her hair, loosening the braid. He tilted her face up and she hungrily, breathlessly, awaited the depth of his kiss.

Instead, he murmured, "Open your eyes, angel."

She did. His face was hazed with passion, his eyes deep and brilliant.

She whispered, "Why do you call me that?"

"Because that's what you are to me." A faint smile deepened one corner of his lips. "The exact opposite of me."

She struggled to bring her breathing back under control, but it wasn't easy. She felt as though nothing but her grip on his waist—and the support of his hands against the back of her neck—kept her from sinking to an inchoate puddle on the floor.

She managed, searching his eyes, "Opposites attract."

Again the smile, deep in his eyes now, and it made her heart swell and quicken.

"So they say."

He leaned down and placed a kiss on the corner of her lips and another against her cheekbone. She drank in his kisses as though they were raindrops and she were dying of thirst.

She lifted her hand then and touched his face, letting her fingers drift through the thick silk of his hair. He had a beautiful face. It was the kind of face dreams were made of . . . jungle dreams, perhaps.

She smiled a little. "You didn't say it."

He turned his face to her caress. "Didn't say what?"

"That I'm beautiful."

He kissed her palm. "I was trying to think of something more original."

"Most men say that, first thing," she said slowly, a little surprised by the course of her own thoughts. She looked at him, hesitant to put it into words yet unable to stay silent. "You said I liked you because you were flamboyant and dangerous and exciting, but that's not it. I like you because you didn't say I was beautiful. You said I was interesting. I don't think any man has ever said that to me before."

He looked at her for a long moment and though his smile didn't fade, something changed subtly in the depths of his eyes. It might have been puzzlement or uncertainty, or something else she was entirely too inexperienced to read. He murmured, "You're starting to sound serious, angel."

Savannah's voice was breathless, a little unsteady. "Maybe I am. I tend to get serious when I'm about to make love with a man."

Again there was a quickening in his eyes. "Is that what we're about to do?"

Her heart was beating so hard she could barely form the whisper. "I think so."

But slowly unmistakably, she felt his retreat. He looked at her with tenderness and regret, and after a long moment, he leaned forward and kissed her on the forehead.

"Thanks for the use of the garden, angel," he said.

He stepped away from her, and he left.

Six

_____

"Well, there haven't been any more burglaries, I'll give him that much," Savannah said.

Detective Jenkins nodded. "Word would have gotten out that you'd brought in an expert. That would be enough to scare off the amateurs."

Savannah shot him a sidelong glance. "That's what he said."

The two of them were walking through the lobby of The Boheme.

She said, keeping her voice as casual as she could, "So, tell me the truth. What do you think of him?"

"Cassidy? How many times are you going to grill me on that guy?"

Savannah refused to be embarrassed. "We have a lot at stake," she reminded the policeman.

She should have said *she* had a lot at stake. Over a week had passed since C. J. Cassidy had broken into her bedroom, fixed her breakfast, almost made love to her and vanished. During that time, she had seen him so rarely that on more than one occasion she had wondered if he still worked there. When she did see him, it was only in passing and there was never a hint of anything that wasn't professional in their exchange. The truth was that Savannah wasn't sure what *she* thought of him at this point...except that as a man he grew more frustrating, and as a mystery more fascinating, every day.

"Besides," she added, "you've given me background, references, facts. You've never given me an opinion. I want your instinct."

He gave a small grunt. What that signified, Savannah couldn't guess.

"Sweetheart, you're talking to a guy who's been a cop for almost thirty years. My *instinct* is that guys like Cassidy give me a bellyache."

Savannah felt a sinking sensation in her own stomach. "Oh? Why is that?"

He shrugged. "They're too smart for their own good. They're too used to playing the odds, and too good at it. Sooner or later, the temptation's going to grab them again, just to see if they can beat the odds one more time. It's like an addiction with them."

Savannah said carefully, "You don't believe in rehabilitation, I take it."

He chuckled. "When it's the self-made kind? No, I can't say that I do. Now, personally, I like Cassidy, and he's one of the best in the business at what he does. I'd recommend him to anybody who asked, yet I wouldn't trust him out of my sight. Does that make any sense to you?"

Savannah sighed. "Unfortunately, it does."

He gave her a quick look that made her suspect his detective instincts were putting together a picture of her interest in Cassidy that was far more accurate than she would have liked. She tried to rearrange her expression into one of professional detachment.

"What really happened to make him change the side of the law he worked on?" she asked. "Do you know?"

"A couple of things. First, he got into a little trouble in Belgium with an undercover agent."

"I thought he'd never been caught."

Jenkins looked momentarily uncomfortable. "Well, technically he hasn't been. But they had enough on him to make him real interested in working a deal. The reason he never faced charges was that he helped the police put away a whole gang of thugs—and he worked a smart deal."

"You said there were a couple of things," Savannah prompted.

The furrow in Jenkin's forehead was thoughtful. "Yeah. The other thing is something he doesn't talk about, but if you ask me, it's the real reason he took that deal. There was this guy, Pete Tobias.''

"Toby," Savannah said softly.

He shot her another quick look. "Right. Toby kind of took Cassidy under his wing, taught him everything he knew, took care of him. I guess you could say he was the only father the kid had ever known. Of course, he was as crooked as a country road, but still, honor among thieves and all that. Anyway, he was killed during one of his jobs. They say Cassidy took it real hard, and it was right after they told him about Tobias that he got involved with Interpol. He's been on our side of the fence ever since."

Savannah remembered describing Cassidy as glamorous, daring, exciting, the stuff of which adventure movies were made. He was all that, but he was also more. And as much as she tried to resist, everything she learned about him only fascinated her more.

"Anyway you're right, he's doing a hell of a job here," Detective Jenkins went on. "There's still a chance, of course, that your burglar might resurface now that the busy season is underway, or that we might turn up something that will lead us to uncover his identity. But if you want my best guess, I'd say the excitement is over for now."

As though on cue, the front doors burst open and an entourage that might best be compared to Cleopatra's entrance into Rome paraded through. Six liveried men pushing luggage racks led the way, followed by two secretaries and a personal maid. Behind them came three nattily dressed young men pushing carts of flowers and behind them another string of attendants carrying trunks, cases and cartons.

Toward the rear of the procession was a wheeled cart supporting a display cage. The cage was decorated with blue velvet draperies, which were looped back to reveal a very snooty-looking lilac-point Himalayan cat. The cat's name, according to the flowing script atop the cage, was indeed Cleopatra. She bore absolutely no resemblance to that sleek historical personage, however, but she almost could have been taken for the twin of the rather plump, fluffy, fur-swathed lady who, with an appropriate flare for drama, brought up the rear.

"Good Lord," exclaimed Detective Jenkins, taking a startled step backward. "Royalty?"

"Not quite." Savannah smiled ruefully. "Emily Bouvier. Excuse me, Detective, it's back to work for me."

Detective Jenkins took another look at the extravagantly dressed woman and the jewel cases and hatboxes and coat boxes piling up around the front desk, and he murmured, "For both of us."

Savannah straightened the hem of her short linen jacket, smoothed her hair, adjusted the bangles on her wrist and went forward with her hands extended and her warmest smile in place.

"Mrs. Bouvier. How lovely to see you again. And Cleopatra, of course." She gave a gracious nod of welcome in the direction of the cage. The Boheme did not generally allow pets, but for a guest as wealthy as Emily Bouvier, they would have assigned the cat its own room and let it open a line of credit.

"There you are, my dear! And how sweet of you to arrange such perfect weather for me. The flight from New York was ghastly, just ghastly, but the minute I stepped off the plane in Miami, I felt an aura start to clear. By the time we reached the island, I was absolutely sparkling!"

"You certainly do appear to be sparkling," Savannah assured her, trying to unobtrusively retrieve her hands from the other woman's crushing grip. On one finger, Emily Bouvier was wearing a ruby that was easily five carats, surrounded by a collection of diamonds that reached almost to her knuckles; on another, she was wearing a gaudy concoction of sapphires, diamonds and rubies that looked heavy enough to weigh down her plump hand. Both rings were cutting into Savannah's fingers quite painfully.

"My dear, it's the air, I swear it. Negative ions, don't you know—or is it positive? I never can keep that straight."

For a moment, her round, much-powdered-and-rouged face formed itself into a puzzled pout, but cleared almost immediately into a high, bell-like laugh. "Well, what difference does it make? The point is I feel marvelous and it's all because I'm back in the sun and clear air of my little home away from home. I really don't know why I don't just buy a place here," she confided, releasing her grip of Savannah's aching fingers at last and linking her arm through the younger woman's, instead. "I'm never quite so happy any-place else as I am at The Boheme."

"And that's exactly why we hope you never buy a place here," Savannah replied. The voluminous white fur coat her guest wore was shedding—as naturally it would in this climate—and it tickled Savannah's nose. She tried not to sneeze as she led the woman toward the elevator bank, and she couldn't help thinking how horrified her environmentally conscious parents would be at the sight of the fur. "No one could ever spoil you the way it's our pleasure to do at The Boheme. It would break our hearts if we should lose you to some cold impersonal private mansion."

Again Emily laughed, and gave Savannah a reprov-ing tap on the arm. Her luxuriant silver hair was al-most an exact match to her arctic fox coat; the silver-blue silk scarf and gloves she wore made her resem-blance to her cat uncanny. Savannah had met the cat, however, and had discovered to her relief that Emily was by far the more pleasant of the two.

"You are a sweet liar," she declared, "but you're exactly right—I would simply expire of ennui if I didn't have all you dear things to fuss and fawn over me."

"Your suite is ready, Mrs. Bouvier," Savannah said. "And we've arranged for massage at three, followed by a body wrap and sauna in the fitness center. And the groomer will arrive at four from Miami to clip Cleopatra's claws."

"Marvelous, my dear, you've thought of everything. No wonder I keep coming back."

"Mrs. Bouvier." From across the lobby, Greg Walker approached, his warmest, most professional smile in place. "Welcome. You're looking stunning as usual."

Emily Bouvier abandoned Savannah for the attentions of a flattering male. "Why, Gregory, my dear, you always make me feel just like a girl!"

It was with a certain amount of relief that Savannah turned her charge over to her boss. She felt a hundred pounds lighter as she stepped back and allowed Greg Walker to escort Emily Bouvier to the elevator.

"A groomer from Miami to clip the cat's claws?" murmured an incredulous voice at her shoulder. "Who the hell *is* that?"

Savannah recognized the voice without turning around, and its proximity caused her heart to skip a beat. But her voice was calm and professional as she replied, "That was Mrs. Emily Bouvier, one of the ten wealthiest women in the world."

Also, Savannah thought but did not add, *one of the biggest security risks a hotel could face.* Even before the burglaries, she had been nervous about the amounts of cash and jewelry Mrs. Bouvier left casually lying around; now, she seemed less like a treasured guest than a security nightmare come true.

Nonetheless, she added casually, "Naturally, we're anxious to keep her happy."

"I'll bet. Did you see the size of those rocks she was wearing?"

"We all did, Cassidy." Detective Jenkins stepped forward, and his tone, though perfectly pleasant, seemed to hold a hint of warning.

Cassidy turned an amused glance on him. "Why, Don, old friend. Do I detect a trace of suspicion in your voice?"

"Not at all, old friend." Though he was smiling, he emphasized the last two words in what was not a particularly friendly way. "It's just that sometimes one of the most effective things a law officer can do to deter crime is just to let the criminals know someone is watching. But you know that, don't you?"

In light of her previous conversation with Detective Jenkins, Savannah did not find this exchange especially amusing.

"Oh, my dear," Mrs. Bouvier called from the elevator, waving to her, "come up to my suite this afternoon and I'll read your palm! I've discovered I have the gift!"

Savannah smiled and waved back, her bracelets jangling with a gaiety she was far from feeling. She held the smile until the doors closed, and then she let her shoulders sag.

"Palm?" inquired Cassidy. "She's a palm reader?"

"Oh, she's always dabbling in fortune-telling and ghost-hunting and whatnot," Savannah replied. Her attention was on the chaos surrounding the desk. The piles of luggage and milling attendants, not to mention the cat, looked to her like a riot waiting to happen.

Detective Jenkins said cheerily, "Well, I see you've got everything under control, so I'll be on my way."

Savannah shot him a dark look, but he just grinned and edged past the mounds of trunks and cartons toward the door.

"I don't believe that woman."

Savannah turned back to the piles of cases and paraphernalia in front of the desk. "How'd you like to be rich enough to walk off and leave a fortune in designer gowns and jewelry and furs piled up in some hotel lobby without even looking back? I mean, will you look at all this? And who knows what might be inside those suitcases?"

"A fortune in jewelry and designer gowns, probably," Cassidy said mildly. And then, to her astonishment, he took a small walkie-talkie from his pocket and said, "Stan, you'd better send another man out here until we get the lobby cleared out. We've got enough capital sitting around in this luggage to finance a small nation, and the desk is pretty busy. Let's meet in Mrs. Bouvier suite in fifteen minutes."

It was then that Savannah realized two of the men who were milling round were members of the hotel's security staff, and they weren't milling at all—they were guarding. She looked at Cassidy in astonishment. "You *do* have things under control, don't you?"

He held up a finger for silence and switched to another channel on the radio device. "Time is of the essence, Mr. Silver," he murmured into it, and across the lobby Savannah saw Roger Silver, the bell captain, lift his hand in acknowledgement. Almost instantaneously, another three bellmen appeared and began loading luggage onto the elevators.

Cassidy looked at Savannah. "You sound surprised."

She shook her head and repressed an exasperated sigh. "Nothing you do surprises me, Mr. Cassidy. I'm beginning to believe you are the most completely unfathomable man I've ever known."

"Most men would be flattered to hear that. Why do I think what you just said was not a compliment?"

Savannah opened her mouth to retort, but she could feel herself being drawn into one of those verbal sparring matches from which she had no chance of emerging a winner. She said, instead, "Why don't you just continue to do your job, and I'll do mine?"

"That," he replied, "is the smartest thing you've said since I met you."

She had half turned to go, but that stopped her. "And just what do you mean by that?"

"It seems fairly self-explanatory to me."

He tucked the walkie-talkie into his pocket and watched the last of the Bouvier parade make its way onto an elevator. Savannah couldn't help noticing that the dispersal had been accomplished in record time.

She took a step toward him, lowering her voice so as not to be overhead in the now relatively quiet lobby. "I certainly hope you're not implying that I've been anything but completely professional in my treatment of you."

"Of course you have," he replied easily. "You've been everything but professional from the minute we met. You've plotted to have me dismissed, you've had me investigated by the police, you've tried to align the employees against me, you've refused to cooperate and you've done everything in your power to make my job as difficult as possible—all because you can't deal with your attraction to me. I'd call that unprofessional, wouldn't you?"

Savannah's mouth dropped open in outrage and astonishment. She didn't know which issue to address first—his absurd accusations, or the incredible conclusion he had drawn from them. Attraction? Unprofessional? Refusal to cooperate? How dare he! She literally struggled with words for several moments and found she couldn't make a sound.

As a bell from the elevator bank chimed to indicate the arrival of an empty elevator, he glanced at his watch and added in that same polite tone, "Excuse me, I have an appointment."

She caught up with him in three strides and accompanied him into the elevator in turbulent silence. Not until the door closed did she burst out, "Me? *I'm* unprofessional? Who was the one who broke into my office and—and—took unfair advantage of me while

I was asleep? Who was it who broke into my *house?* And I did *not* have you investigated by the police.''

''I know, Jenkins gave you that one as a favor.''

If she hadn't been so infuriated she might have noticed the curve of his lips, the glint of his eye that indicated he was enjoying this far more than he should have. But she was beyond noticing anything except the enormous satisfaction of venting a week's worth of frustration and confusion and having the excuse of his unjustified attack as provocation.

''And let's just talk for a minute about who can't deal with what attraction!'' she went on angrily, balling up her fists. ''I didn't walk out on you, you may recall!''

''Biggest mistake I ever make,'' he admitted, and in one easy movement he turned and gathered her into his arms.

Savannah didn't even have time to draw a startled breath. His mouth covered hers, his tongue penetrated her, heat and dizziness surged and she melted into him. His fingers pressed hard into her buttocks, then moved lower, stroking the shape of her hip and her thigh and finding the hemline of her short linen skirt, caressing the flesh of her stocking-covered upper leg.

Savannah swallowed back a moan as the passion flared. Helplessly she pressed herself into him, winding her leg around his, caressing his calf with her ankle. He tasted of wintergreen and sea breezes and all things masculine and untamed. That taste infused her, drugged her, filled her with a surprising rush of un-controlled longing. Surprising, perhaps, not because of its suddenness, but because of its intensity.

Dimly she heard the chime of the elevator bells an-nouncing their next stop. Cassidy dragged his mouth away from hers, and his breath was hot and moist on her neck. The sensation caused a tightening deep in her belly, one last swift clutch of desire.

"What are you doing?" she whispered. "I thought we were having a fight."

"Just being unpredictable," he assured her huski-ly. His tongue delved into the hollow of her collar-bone, making her shiver with delight.

"You are insane," she gasped, clinging to him when she knew she should be pushing away.

He pressed a last deep and drawing kiss over the center of her throat. "And don't you forget it," he murmured.

The doors slid open and Savannah pushed herself quickly away, breathing hard. She spent a frantic mo-ment smoothing her hair and straightening her jacket and tugging at the hem of her skirt while Cassidy, as cool as an autumn day, smiled and held the elevator door for her.

Her head was roaring as she stepped out into the corridor, her nerves a jumble of misfires and raw sen-sation, like a tangle of bare wires tossed into a heap on the floor. It did not even occur to her to wonder where they were or why she was here until they reached the end of the corridor, where the double doors stood open on the cheerful chaos of the Bouvier suite.

Greg Walker was there, as was Stan Keller, half a dozen bellmen and two maids. Emily ordered them all around with a gay disregard for rank or class, completely in her element. Trunks and suitcases were open and their contents spread over the furniture or spilled onto the floor. All that glitter and silk added a Mardis Gras atmosphere to the general disorder, and it was enough to drag Savannah's attention away from the tumultuous events in the elevator and onto the pandemonium of the present.

"Darling, darling, come in!" Emily lifted a plump arm and waved Savannah over. "You can help me decide what to wear tonight. Did I tell you Wallace is driving down for dinner? Something nice, of course, but not too overstated."

"No tiaras tonight, then, hmm?" Savannah managed to glue her smile in place as she crossed the room.

That seemed to inspire Emily into recollection, and she gasped with childlike delight as she scrambled among the bags and boxes on the floor. "I must show you my latest! It's simply too darling for words."

Savannah could practically feel the two security men wince as she brought up a jewelry case that had been haphazardly deposited among the other things on the floor, and flipped it open. The case had not even been locked.

"Mrs. Bouvier." Cassidy stepped forward as she rummaged through the sparkling tangle of rings and brooches and chains. "Please allow me to introduce myself. My name is C. J. Cassidy and I've been hired by the hotel as a security consultant."

Emily's look of annoyance faded into one of unabashed appreciation as she looked up. "My," she said, extending her hand to him, "you are good-looking, aren't you?"

Cassidy smiled and bowed over her hand. Emily practically purred.

"Well-mannered, too," she murmured. Her eyes enjoyed Cassidy as though he were a rich dessert. "What did you say your job was, young man?"

Stan stepped forward, clearing his throat brusquely. "What I'm sure Mr. Cassidy intended to suggest, ma'am, was that you might be more comfortable putting those lovely jewels of yours into the hotel safe."

"Nonsense," replied Emily breezily, removing her attention from Cassidy and retrieving her hand with obvious reluctance. "Why in the world would I have carted this lot all the way from New York only to bury it in some dismal safe? No, indeed, the only fun of having jewels is in wearing them, and I'm sure this nice young man would agree, wouldn't you, dear?"

Cassidy replied smoothly, "Indeed, I would. And a woman as lovely as you should never be without adornment. However, since one can only wear so many jewels at one time, it might be prudent to keep the rest in a safe place."

Emily turned to Savannah, her eyes snapping with pleasure. "My dear, if this were a department store, I'd order ten of him. Isn't he the most priceless thing?" She turned and thrust the jewelry box into Cassidy's hands, adding, "This isn't the right case at all. Now, where did I put...?"

Savannah could not help noticing the way Cassidy's eyes moved over the contents of the box, inventorying, assaying and coming up with a total as quickly and efficiently as a cash register. The professional assessment was performed with a kind of second nature that Savannah couldn't help but find unsettling, and apparently she wasn't the only one.

Stan stepped forward deliberately and took the box from Cassidy. "I'll just see this gets to the safe," he said.

Cassidy smiled. "Of course."

"Here it is!" declared Emily. Triumphantly, she emerged from a tower of bandboxes with her hair slightly rumpled and her hands proudly clutching a narrow tapestry-covered case. "Can you imagine? I thought I had left it behind."

Without further ado, she flipped open the box and displayed the necklace inside for all to see.

It was the most stunning collection of emeralds and diamonds that Savannah had ever seen—not that she had had the opportunity to see that many emerald-and-diamond necklaces. The centerpiece was a forest-rich, sharply cut emerald as big as a half-dollar, supported by a gold floral design that was studded, in random patterns where the leaves fell, with tiny, perfectly cut diamonds. The chain was also a floral design, with smaller emeralds and diamonds forming the petals. The workmanship was so fine, the stones so perfect, that even though there was enough glitter in that box to make a person squint even with sunglasses, the effect was breathtaking, not gaudy.

"Isn't it exquisite?" asked Emily beaming. "It was designed by Phillipe Marquet, one of the most famous designers in the business. He wins all sorts of prizes. It has a fascinating history, too. Parts of it are quite antique. I'm told the emeralds were once part of a necklace that was given to—"

"Josephine Bonaparte," murmured Cassidy in an odd, almost reverent tone, "as a wedding gift."

Savannah stared at him. She had never seen such a look of raw, unabashed lust on any man's face before. Every feminine instinct within her prickled with jealousy even as her more rational side sharpened into alertness—and more than a little uneasiness.

Emily Bouvier looked surprised, then approving. "Why, yes! I knew you were a gentlemen of refinement and education the moment I saw you."

Cassidy said, without ever taking his gaze off the necklace, "May I hold it?"

She didn't hesitate. "Why, of course, my dear." She removed the necklace from its box and said rather smugly to Stan, "You see, *this* is what beautiful things were meant for—to be enjoyed, not locked away in a safe where no one can ever see them."

She draped the necklace across Cassidy's fingers. He accepted it with a mixture of awe and sensual delight that was fascinating to watch. He let the necklace drift through his fingers like liquid, pooling it in his palm, caressing each stone with luxuriant absorption, as though memorizing its curves with his fingertips. Watching him, Savannah could not help but be reminded of the magic those long sensitive fingers played on her own flesh, and again she felt that curious mixture of jealousy and excitement.

"This is," he said at last, huskily, "a magnificent piece of work. You're to be congratulated on owning it, madame."

Emily practically glowed. "I'm terribly proud of it, you know. I'm just like a child when I get something new—can't wait to show it off."

"I can certainly understand why you'd want to show off something this beautiful," Cassidy agreed.

"But surely, Mrs. Bouvier," Savannah interjected quickly, "you weren't thinking of wearing it tonight."

The older woman's brow drew into a V of puzzlement. "Shouldn't I?"

"Oh, I'd think you would want to save it for a special occasion," Savannah insisted. Just being near something as rare and expensive as that necklace was causing her skin to prickle with nervous perspiration, and she could tell Greg Walker felt the same way.

"Indeed," Greg agreed. "A necklace like that definitely deserves a special occasion for its showcase.

And in the meantime, I really do think you would be wise to let us keep it for you in the safe."

Savannah saw the objection forming and stepped in before it could be voiced. "Mrs. Bouvier, please. That necklace has got to be worth close to a million dollars—"

"It's worth 2.3 million, to be precise," Cassidy said softly.

Savannah looked at him sharply. He was still holding the necklace, still caressing it.

"And our room safes simply aren't designed for that kind of security," Savannah went on, a little desperately.

"Oh, bother," Emily said peremptorily. "I never use those silly things." She looked at Cassidy shrewdly. "What would *you* have me do, young man?"

Cassidy raised his eyes to her, and smiled. "Mrs. Bouvier, it's your necklace. You have every right to enjoy it as you please." He returned the necklace to her with obvious reluctance and went on, "But something this rare, this beautiful . . . well, it almost demands an extra measure of care, doesn't it? If I had a classic car, I would park it in a heated garage when I wasn't using it. If I had a vintage bottle of wine, I would keep it in a temperature-controlled wine cellar. Can you do anything less for a piece of art as magnificent as this?"

Emily Bouvier gave him a smile that indicated his charm would only go so far, and replied, "Since I don't suppose you're suggesting I should keep my necklace in a cellar..." With an elaborate sigh she returned the piece of jewelry to its box and snapped the lid closed. "Very well. Take it to your dusty old safe."

She handed the box to Stan and it seemed that the entire room breathed a collective sigh of relief.

"You're doing the right thing, Mrs. Bouvier," Stan said. "I'll take these jewels down to the safe now and bring you a receipt."

"Yes, you do that." Her moment of grief having passed, Emily's attention had already moved on to another subject. "Do you know I believe I'll wear the gold lamé tonight, and you're quite right, my dear, the emeralds wouldn't do with it at all."

"Madame, it's been a pleasure," Cassidy said, and Greg Walker added, "Let me know if there's anything you need, anything at all..."

Now that the matter of the necklace had been resolved, everyone who was not expecting a tip was trying to make his escape. Greg and Cassidy made it, and Savannah had almost reached the door when Emily chimed out, "Oh, darling, don't hurry out. We've plenty of time for your reading now, just come over here and sit down."

"Oh, I really hate to bother you when you've just arrived," Savannah protested, continuing to edge for the door. "Maybe later."

"Nonsense, I'm at my best in an atmosphere of activity and accomplishment."

"But you haven't even unpacked, and Cleopatra is expecting the manicurist."

"Come here," commanded Emily Bouvier with an imperious wave, and Savannah had no choice but to obey.

"Just a quick peek," added Emily with a little giggle as she took Savannah over to the window where the light was the strongest. "I confess I'm curious to see . . . aha! I was right!"

Triumphantly, she held Savannah's hand palm up, pointing toward the center of it. "It's that delightful young man, just as I suspected. Why, if you're not careful, he'll steal your heart away before you know it!"

Savannah was staring, not at her palm, but at her wrist. Her lips tightened, and she closed her hand slowly. "It's not my heart I'm worried about," she muttered.

She pulled her hand away and forced a smile. "Excuse me, Mrs. Bouvier. I have to catch a thief."

And, leaving the astonished lady to gape after her, Savannah marched out the door.

Seven

She caught up with Cassidy at the elevator. He was, unfortunately, standing with a group of guests and talking to Greg Walker. She forced herself to take a calming breath and painted a polite smile on her face.

"Oh, Mr. Cassidy. I wonder if I might have a word with you?"

He inclined his head toward her. "Of course."

He waited for her to speak. So did the group of guests. So did Greg Walker. It was very difficult to keep smiling.

"In private?" she suggested tightly.

He glanced at his watch, as though he might have something better to do. As though it would matter if he did. "I've got a few minutes. My office?"

The elevator chimed, the door slid open.

"Fine," she said.

People started to file onto the elevator, and Savannah couldn't help thinking about the last elevator ride she'd taken with Cassidy. She didn't know whether to be relieved or disappointed that this one would not be so private.

Cassidy held the door for her from outside the elevator as she stepped on. "Where is your office?" she asked.

"Suite 300," he replied, and released the doors.

Savannah stepped off the elevator just before the doors slid shut. They were on the third floor.

"Very funny," she said.

He grinned and reached for her hand, holding it palm up. Her bangles made a cheery tinkling sound as he dropped them into her hand.

Savannah closed her fingers around the bracelets and took a calming breath. "Why do you keep doing that?" she demanded.

He quirked an eyebrow at her as he led the way toward his suite. "Because it's so easy?"

"I mean it." She slipped the bracelets back on her wrist, confronting him as they reached the door to his suite. "They weren't even real gold, for heaven's sake!"

He smiled and slipped his hand around her neck, caressing it briefly. "Because," he explained simply, "I don't want you to forget who I am."

"Small chance of that," Savannah muttered, but his touch, brief though it was, had left a tingle of warmth on her skin that was difficult to ignore.

He inserted his card into the lock and the lock clicked open on the first try. Savannah had heard nothing but rave reviews on the new key-card system.

He pushed open the door and glanced back at her. "Was that all?"

Savannah hesitated, then squared her shoulders. "No, Mr. C. J. Cassidy. That is not all."

She stepped into the room.

The suite was not quite as large or as luxurious as the one assigned to Emily Bouvier, but it was more than adequate for someone who was, essentially, an employee of the hotel. He had transformed the outer room into an office that rivaled only Greg Walker's for its comfort and luxury. The brocaded furniture had been rearranged to divide the room into two separate spaces: one somewhat informal with the television, bar and sofa; the other, transformed by the addition of a conference table and a file cabinet, contained a personal computer, two telephones and several armchairs drawn up in the traditional interview position near the desk. The desk itself was set close to the sliding glass doors, which opened onto a private balcony and a spectacular view of the ocean.

The door to the bedroom was kept closed, but Savannah knew—because she knew every room in this hotel—that it contained a king-size bed, access to another balcony and a luxurious bathroom with heated towel racks and a Jacuzzi. As far as fringe benefits go, he could have done worse.

She said, glancing around, "Very impressive. And how convenient—right down the hall from your biggest fan."

"Jealousy doesn't become you."

He crossed the room and opened the balcony doors partway. The distant roar of the ocean and the fresh sea breeze tumbled in.

"If I were inclined to be jealous," Savannah couldn't help retorting, "I'd have good reason, and it wouldn't have anything to do with your accommodations, either."

"Oh?" He turned to look at her. "What then?"

He stood before the desk, leaning one hip against it as he casually glanced through a stack of mail. The flood of sunlight from the balcony touched off redgold highlights in his hair and backlit his slender body with a soft white aura. Upon entering the suite, he had shrugged off his jacket and loosened his tie. Now he stood before her in a crisp white shirt and gray trousers, looking good enough to eat.

She already regretted having spoken, but she didn't seem to be able to avoid an answer to his question. She replied, frowning, "Let's just say I'd be willing to bet you've never looked at a woman the way you looked at Emily Bouvier's necklace."

He tossed the stack of mail aside, his eyes gently amused.

"Then you must not have been paying very close attention to the way I look at you."

She hadn't expected him to say that. But then, she never knew *what* to expect from him. She felt heat creep into her face and she tried to swallow it back. Her fingers closed into fists but it was not an angry gesture, rather it was a strengthening one. With a lift of her chin she steeled herself against his smile, his eyes, his charm.

"This is not a joking matter," she told him sharply.

"What makes you think I'm joking?"

"How did you know so much about that necklace?" she demanded. "You acted as though you didn't even know who Emily Bouvier was, but one look at that necklace and you could recite its history and its market value without even thinking hard. How did you know?"

The humor gradually faded from his eyes, although his casual demeanor did not alter in any other way. "I read," he replied negligently. "Part of the job."

"*Which* job?" she snapped, and was instantly sorry.

The remoteness that came into his eyes chilled her to the bone. He no longer pretended to be having a friendly conversation.

"Why do you care?" he returned coolly. "I really don't think this is within your—"

"You *know* why I care!"

"Ah, yes, the ever-vigilant watchdog." His tone had an edge to it now, his eyes were like ice picks. "You can't afford to take any chances when it comes to your hotel, can you?"

"It has nothing to do with the hotel!" she cried. A muffled sound of frustration escaped her throat and she thrust her fingers into her hair, half turning from him. "God, you make me crazy! I never know when to trust you or believe you or even take you seriously! Why can't you once, just once, be straight with me?"

Momentary surprise flickered over his eyes and he took a half step forward. Then he stopped and settled back as his expression arranged itself into the familiar cynical lines. "You're better off not trusting me, angel. And God knows, you should never take me seriously."

Savannah faced him squarely, her heart beating hard. "Is that why you walked out on me the other day?"

He didn't answer for a moment. They stood a little over four feet apart, and the distance between them seemed at the same time as great as a chasm and so small it could be closed with a breath. Inside Savannah's head, the voice of reason demanded incredulously, *What are you doing? Why are you pushing this? Back away, for heaven's sake, get out while you still can.*

But the air between them was electric with expectation and she knew exactly why she was doing this. It was already too late to back away.

He said softly, "What do you think would have happened if I had stayed?"

All she could see was the way the light sparked in his hair and planed his face with golden shadows. All she could feel was his gaze, caressing her again, stroking her face, her throat, her breasts, her abdomen, arousing her without a touch, drawing her close, setting her on fire.

She said, "We would have made love."

His gaze returned to her face. She thought she could see the tensing of his muscles beneath the fine weave of his shirt, and though his expression remained placid, there seemed to be a cautious question in his eyes, a searching.

He said huskily, "Then I did you a favor by leaving. Didn't I?"

Though she tried to keep her voice steady, her reply was a little breathless. "Did you?"

She could count the seconds by the beats of her heart, yet each one seemed longer, more wrenched with expectation and uncertainty, than the one before. And then he moved toward her.

Outside, a sea gull squawked. A gust of warm wind flapped the heavy drapery like a sail and rifled papers on the desk. Savannah stood still, and he filled her vision, coming closer. Her heart pounded so hard it shook the tiny gold pin fastened to her lapel.

Cassidy fastened his hands on her waist, pulling her close, thigh against thigh, belly against belly. He bent his head close to hers and she thought he would kiss her; already she was helpless to resist his power. His eyes were polished stones, and the gleam within them was like a distant flame; it pierced her skin and heated her blood.

But when his mouth was close enough to drink her in, he spoke. "What do you want from me, Savannah?" he demanded huskily. His breath brushed her parted lips. "A chance to impress your hippie parents? A little walk on the wild side? A chance to say you lived dangerously, just once—and survived to tell the tale?"

Her heart was pounding even harder, making her breath shudder and tightening her throat, all but robbing her of her voice. "Maybe," she whispered. With all the will she possessed, she stood straight in his arms, she met his gaze. "Maybe all of those. Maybe... more."

The muscles of his arms hardened. "I can't give you any more, angel." His eyes were dark and intent, and he looked at her as though trying to physically imprint his words on her brain. "Don't expect anything more from me, do you understand? This is all there is."

She said, "You're wrong."

His hands tightened on her waist and she thought he would push her away; perhaps that was what he meant to do. Instead, he moved a fraction closer, as though drawn by an invisible magnet. His lips brushed hers; he seemed to breathe the words into her mouth. "Don't trust me."

Dizziness prickled at her, she steadied herself by pressing her hands flat against his chest. "I won't," she whispered.

His tongue flicked at the inside of her lips, tasting her. "Don't depend on me."

"All right." Savannah's eyes drifted closed as she felt the heat and pressure of his kiss on her throat; it went through her like molten honey.

"Don't try to change me," he whispered, tasting her collarbone and the curve of her jaw. "And for God's sake, don't fall in love with me."

"I won't."

His mouth sought hers and she rose to meet him, hungrily, greedily, and with a kind of desperate savagery that surprised even her. Her fingers pressed into the hard muscles of his chest and slid upward, over his shoulders, around his biceps. The tactile sensation of soft cotton shielding hard, heated flesh made her palms tingle and she ached to know more of him, to memorize every inch of him with her hands. His hands moved up, pushing beneath her jacket to caress her back, then pressing against the back of her neck, his fingers thrusting into her hair as the force of his kiss bent her head backward.

He tore his mouth away, breathing hard. He braced her face between his hands and searched her eyes intently, a fever in his own. "Angel," he said hoarsely, "I haven't been able to get you out of my head since I left you the other morning, and every time I think about you, my blood feels like it's on fire. If you don't stop me now, we're both going to be in a lot of trouble.''

She whispered, "I know."

And instead of stepping away as any sensible person would have done—as any rational, sane and responsible person should have done—Savannah encircled his neck with her arms and sought his mouth again.

It was crazy. She knew it was crazy. It was the middle of a workday and they both were on duty. The phone could ring or a knock could come at the door any moment, but knowing that did not sober her as it should have done; the flames only surged higher. Was danger his allure? Adventure, excitement, risk...that was all part of it, she was sure. But she had not lied before; there was more, and it was the more she was hungry for, desperate for, that she could not bear to miss.

She worked the buttons of his shirt, pushing her hand inside. Her fingers tangled in the mat of damp silky hair and spread over the hard swell of his pectoral muscle. She opened her mouth against his face, tasting the heat and the roughness, sliding down to his throat and collarbone, inhaling him.

His hands caressed her hips and thighs, pushing up her skirt, tracing the line of her panties beneath her hose. His breath was hot on her face, long and slow but unsteady. His heart beat like an anvil hammer against her palm.

"Don't be sorry," he whispered. The tingle of heat that rushed across her ear ignited every fiber in her skin and made her knees weak. "I don't want you to be sorry."

She opened his shirt another button, pressing her lips into the hollow of his throat. "I'm not," she whispered.

He grasped both of her hands in his and brought them to his lips. Savannah's breath stopped in her throat, first from surprise and then from pleasure as he opened her hands one by one, to the caress of his lips. He lowered her arms slowly to her sides, holding her still with his eyes as he tugged the sleeves of her jacket off her shoulders, over her arms and let it fall to the floor.

He did the same with her shirt, and then the short pleated skirt. She was trembling as she stood before him in silky chemise and panties, but not from cold. He lifted his hands to cup her breasts, then covered one breast with his mouth, infusing heat and moisture and electric sensation through the thin material into her flesh. Savannah gasped out loud and her knees would no longer support her. Together, they sank to the floor.

She remembered pushing his shirt off his shoulders and unsnapping the button of his trousers. But how or when the remainder of their clothing was discarded she did not know. His hands and his tongue played over her flesh, bringing her to the peak of almost unbearable arousal. Her hands slid across the planes of his chest, cupping his shoulders and the rippling muscles of his back; she tasted the salt on his skin and the satiny texture of his shoulders, the scratchy surface of his chin. She wrapped her legs around his, straining against the pleasure of his touch, aching for him, for the need she felt was powerful and commanding, blotting out all else except the one person who could fulfill it.

He cradled her head with his hands, kissing her face, her eyes, her lips. He whispered her name, and she opened her eyes, seeing his face through a haze of passion and joy. His skin was flushed, his eyes dark and backlit with a gleam of hunger, and on his face was the same expression she had seen when he'd looked at Emily Bouvier's diamond-and-emerald necklace—yet even more intent, more consuming. She let herself drown in that look, surrendering completely to it, and to him, as he gathered her to him.

She felt the low sharp pressure of his entry and she gasped with the exquisite pleasure of their bodies blending, joining, shaping themselves to one another. She arched to meet him and greedily sought his kisses, long and fevered. She clung to him, letting him sink into every pore, every fiber of her being, and the only thing she could clearly think was how right this felt, how very right.

They began to move together, perfectly matched rhythms of mutual need and escalating power. Her entire world narrowed to this man, wild and exciting and tender, mysterious and oddly vulnerable. More

than anything in her life, she wanted to claim him as
her own and to belong to him in turn, to love him...to
be loved by him. The waves of pleasure gathered force
and seemed to expand, sweeping the world, the entire
universe, into the spiral of their power. The explo-
sion, when it came, seemed to shatter the very foun-
dation of her being, cascades of deep soul-wrenching
pleasure that went on and on and left her at last
drained and exhausted and filled with only him.
Where once there were two, now there was one, for
never would she be completely separate from him
again.

She lay in the circle of his arms while the breeze
from the open window cooled their perspiration-
slicked bodies and gradually brought hints of the
world outside—the distant surf, a scrap of laughter,
the screech of seabirds. Savannah let the sounds and
scents drift into her daze of contentment and become
a part of it. She questioned nothing, she asked for
nothing, except that this moment go on and on...
which of course it could not.

The telephone purred twice and was cut off, pre-
sumably by the switchboard or an answering device.
Cassidy did not stir. His arms were warm and strong
around her; the familiar shape of his body molded
hers. His breath sighed into her hair.

She lifted their entwined hands to her lips and kissed
his fingers. Her bracelets jangled as she did so and that

made her smile. She looked at him. "What're you thinking about?"

His smile was drowsy and peaceful, yet distantly sad. He released one of his fingers from their gentle lock with hers and traced the curve of her cheekbone, just beneath her eye. "About how unexpected you are, and fascinating, and, yes, beautiful . . . and what terrible taste you have in men. Ah, angel." And he dropped his eyes, hiding his expression. "What have we done?"

"We've just made love on the floor in the middle of a business day," she replied. "And I somehow doubt that this is the first time that's ever been done in this hotel."

He smiled and turned her face toward his, placing a lingering kiss on her forehead. "You are an incredible woman," he said softly. "And very, very foolish."

"So I've been told."

He looked at her, his eyes searching hers, and his face held uncertainty and reluctance beneath the lingering wonder of what they had just shared. He said, "Savannah . . ."

She knew instinctively she did not want to hear what he was going to say next.

"Tell me a secret, C.J.," she interrupted.

She felt the tension leave his muscles, and his expression momentarily relaxed. "Constantine Justus," he replied. "That's what C.J. stands for. She may not have been much of a mother, but she had a lot of imagination.''

Savannah said gently, ''What happened to Toby?''

The shutter that came down over his eyes was more of surprise than obstinance, and his stiffening was instinctual. Nonetheless, she could see the effort it took for him to open that part of his life to her, to share with her what was obviously so painful to him.

He said, ''He was killed, on a job.''

His voice had that casual, almost-negligent tone that Savannah had come to recognize as one he frequently used to disguise his emotions when the words he spoke were important. He sat up and reached for his pants, offering Savannah his shirt.

Then he said, ''It was a stupid thing, really. A second-story job—they call them that even when the second story is a hundred feet above the ground. He was too damn old for that kind of thing.''

His back was to her, and his voice was gruff. Savannah suspected that he was as surprised as she was to hear himself speaking. Detective Jenkins had said he never talked about it; Savannah wanted him to talk about it to her. And so, apparently, did Cassidy.

''He fell,'' he said. ''Apparently, somebody came in and he had to make a quick escape and—he just fell. He had twenty dollars in his pocket when they found him.''

He pulled his pants over his hips and fastened them. The movements were fluid and easy, but his silence was filled with an unspoken pain perhaps only Savan-

nah could see, and she ached with it. She pushed her
arms into the sleeves of his shirt and drew it around
her, chilled by his absence though he was only a few
inches away.

When he spoke again, his voice was heavy and
thoughtful. "Twenty dollars," he repeated. "He died
for twenty dollars. I guess I realized then that everything he'd taught me, everything we'd done was a
sham, empty...and I didn't want to end up like he had.
But more than that, I realized that the life we'd had—
I'd had—wasn't what I wanted. The things I took were
only pieces of a life, you see, the kind of life I could
never have, one that was quiet and respectable and
stable and secure. I didn't want those pieces anymore. I wanted that *life*. And I guess I finally figured
out that was something you couldn't steal. I've been
working ever since to try to get it—respectability, re-
liability, stability."

And then he turned around to look at her. His gaze
was tender and very sad. "All the things you're either
born with or you're not. All the things you have and I
don't. I can't outlive my past, angel, and you're not
the first one to point that out. But when I'm with you,
I almost think I can. At least you make me want to try.
When I'm with you, I feel more than myself, somehow, better than I am. And that's why, even though I
know I should apologize for what just happened, I'm
not going to. Because I'd be lying if I said I wasn't
glad."

Savannah pressed her head against his shoulder, encircling his waist with her arms. "I'm glad, too," she said softly. "And I don't want you to apologize."

He took her hands firmly in both of his, turning to get a fuller look at her. "I'm glad," he said carefully, "for the memory of something incredible and precious. And you know that's all it can ever be, don't you?"

Savannah felt her heart beating slow and heavy in her chest. *That* was what she hadn't wanted to hear. Yet she wasn't surprised. She knew him better than he suspected; better, perhaps, than she wanted to.

"No," she said. "I don't know that. What I know is that something is starting here and I think it might be the beginning of the only important thing that's ever happened in my life. And I think I deserve a chance to find out. Don't you?"

He dropped his eyes. "Savannah, you know that's not possible. I'm not the kind of man you can depend on. There's no place for me in your life."

She said steadily, "I don't know any of that. All I know is that when I'm with you, I feel alive, more alive than I've ever felt before. I'm not going to let go of that feeling without a fight, C. J. Cassidy."

The telephone buzzed again, and this time his eyes flickered toward it. Savannah said, "I know. I have terrible timing. It's always been one of my faults. But..." She stroked his cheek, trying to coax a smile from him. "I have great taste in men. Nothing is going to be said now that makes any sense, Cassidy.

Come to my house tonight. We'll have dinner. We'll sit in the garden and drink wine and watch the stars. We'll talk. Okay?''

She knew he was going to refuse. She could see it in his eyes. Every muscle in her body, every beat of her heart, willed him to say yes. She didn't breathe, concentrating on her need.

What happened next almost made her a believer in the power of wishes. He took her face in his hands, and he smiled. Very gently, he kissed her lips. "You," he said, "are impossible to resist. Tonight. I'll be there."

And tonight everything would change. She would make certain of it.

One chance was all she asked.

Eight

He didn't come.

Savannah passed the rest of the day in a haze, left work early and spent the remaining hours in a blur of activity, because only by keeping busy could she push back that nagging little voice that kept telling her he wouldn't come.

She shopped for shrimp and fresh-baked bread and exotically scented candles, all the while refusing to remember that look in his eyes that clearly told her he was not coming. She took a long bath and did her nails and curled her hair and tried not to think that he might have been right; that what they had shared together in his suite had been nothing more than a wild and glorious adventure, a moment of unbridled lust now over and best forgotten, and not the most important thing in her life. She dressed in a tiny, form-fitting sundress and shook her hair loose over her shoulders and back. She lit dozens of candles in the courtyard and told herself that he would come; that the final kiss they had shared that afternoon had not been his way of saying goodbye.

She poured the wine, she made the salad, she sat down in the candle-lit garden to wait.

When it grew too chilly to wait outside, she went indoors. She brought the wine with her. A dozen times she went to the phone to call him, and each time she convinced herself to let it go, to leave the man some dignity—to leave *herself* some dignity. Yet, foolishly, forlornly, she waited. She drank more wine. She hoped he would change his mind, see that she was right, find her irresistible, come bursting through the door with some wild tale about traffic jams or muggers or hurricanes. She fell asleep curled up on the sofa with an empty wineglass in her hand, still half hoping.

And that was where she was when the phone woke her the next morning.

The shrilling of the bell pierced her head and the sunlight stabbed at her eyes. The room had the stale smell of melted wax, old wine and abandoned dreams. The burnt-out stubs of candles were everywhere. The shrimp salad was a congealed mess on the kitchen counter. The wine bottle was overturned on the floor. It was the most depressing sight Savannah had ever seen.

And it served her right.

The phone continued to shriek. She fumbled for it, squinting in the morning light, found it at last and croaked, "Hello?"

"Ms. Monterey, what a pleasant surprise." It was Greg Walker's voice, and it did not sound at all pleasant. "Will you be coming into work today or do you have more pressing concerns?"

Savannah looked at her watch and barely suppressed a groan. It was almost eleven o'clock. "I'll be there," she managed to say, struggling to her feet.

"I would appreciate it. And do hurry, will you? There's been something of a crisis and we can use all the help we can get."

And with those words, he disconnected, leaving Savannah's heart pounding with alarm and every sense screeching into alertness. Crisis? What kind of crisis? Could that be why Cassidy hadn't shown up last night? Of course not. Cassidy hadn't shown up last night because he was Cassidy and she was an idiot. But something was wrong and Cassidy was involved; he *had* to be. Was he still there? Had he abandoned not only her but his job and his responsibilities to the hotel? Was *that* the crisis?

She brushed her teeth, splashed water on her face, changed her clothes and was in her car in four minutes. In another five, she pulled recklessly into her parking space and bounded up the steps of the hotel. Her secretary met her at the door and from the look on the other woman's face, Savannah could tell the

growing sense of urgency that had propelled her thus
far was not unjustified.

"They're in Mrs. Bouvier's suite," Holly said. "Mr.
Walker's been calling down here every couple of minutes looking for you. Hurry!"

But Savannah was already running for the elevator,
dread hammering at her heels. The Bouvier suite...she
must have known. All along, she must surely have
known.

The suite was in chaos, as she expected it to be. She
arrived at the open door breathless and windblown,
with her heart pounding in her throat. For a moment,
she could do nothing but try to catch her composure
while surveying the room with a kind of subdued des-
peration for clues to the puzzle, even though she already knew the answer.

She had had time to do no more than catch her hair
back at the nape with an elasticized band, and it hung
free almost to her waist. She was wearing pleated pants
and an oversize cotton jacket, sandals and no stockings; her eyes were puffy, her face was devoid of
makeup and she knew exactly what she must look like
to those who glanced at her.

Detective Jenkins was there, along with two uniformed officers. Stan Keller was there, Art Canon, the
night security chief and Greg Walker. The concierge,
two miserable-looking desk clerks and Emily Bouvier
herself completed the cast. The one person she hoped
to see, desperately longed to see, was not there.

Emily was the last to notice her. She gave a little cry of relief and got to her feet, making her way toward Savannah. "Oh, my dear! Did you hear? Isn't it just the most awful thing?"

She was wearing a voluminous silk mumu printed with cabbage roses and had a pink silk turban on her head. She clutched a rather recalcitrant-looking Cleopatra to her bosom, and Savannah couldn't help noticing the rhinestone collar the cat wore as an exact match to the diamond bracelet on Emily's plump wrist.

Without waiting for a reply, Emily declared, "My necklace, the emerald one—oh, how could I have been so foolish? It's gone! Completely gone!"

Savannah leaned against the door frame for support, taking a deep breath to try to keep her head clear. She didn't know why she was so shocked. And why couldn't she get the memory of the way Cassidy had looked at that necklace out of her head?

Somehow, she managed to make her voice work. Somehow, she actually sounded calm, even reassuring. "But surely, Mrs. Bouvier, you must mean you misplaced it since you took it out of the safe. A two-million-dollar emerald necklace doesn't just disappear." *Not in my hotel,* she prayed silently. *Not with the man I love in charge of it.* But she knew the prayer was futile. Just as the vigil she had kept for him all last night had been.

Emily was already shaking her head. "Why, I didn't have a chance to, not a chance! It was there in your

safe last night when I went down to get my diamonds—I know because I took it out just for a minute to see how it *would* look with the lamé, but you
were right, it needed a quieter background. Then, this
morning, I decided to wear it to luncheon with Wilhelm. The box was there, just where I had left it, but
when I opened it, right here in this room not more
than half an hour ago, it was empty!''

''Why didn't you open the box downstairs?'' Jenkins asked.

She looked at him blankly, and said, ''Why would
I want to?''

Detective Jenkins said, ''And you're sure the box
was never out of your sight after you brought it to the
room?''

''I told you so, didn't I?'' replied Emily in exasperation, and added to Savannah, ''Honestly, I do believe being hard-of-hearing must be a requirement for
the police force these days—I must have answered the
same question a dozen times!''

Without warning, she thrust Cleopatra into Savannah's arms. ''Will you look after her for a moment,
dear? The poor precious thing is so upset by all of this
I'm afraid she may have to go into therapy again. And
these policemen simply will *not* leave me alone.''

Emily departed in a flutter of silk roses to give the
policemen a piece of her mind. Cleopatra dug her
claws into Savannah's shoulder and growled.

Savannah spent a moment trying to disengage cat
claws—which were plenty sharp despite their mani-

cure—from her flesh, while trying to make sense of what Emily had just told her, and trying very hard not to eavesdrop on the conversation she was now having with Stan and Detective Jenkins.

Greg Walker came over to her. "Nice of you to join us, Ms. Monterey. Quite a mess, huh? Still think the hotel business is fun?"

Savannah moved into the room, trying to shift the cat into a more comfortable position. She said desperately, "God, it's not true, is it? The necklace wasn't stolen? How could that have happened?"

"A very interesting question, and one that consumes us all at this moment. It would appear that the necklace was present and accounted for last evening at eight o'clock when Mrs. Bouvier went down to choose her dinner jewelry. But as of ten-thirty this morning, it was gone. I must say I don't like to think what the headlines will do to the tourist season, do you? We both may be looking for jobs before the month is out."

Savannah swallowed hard, dreading to ask the obvious question—where was Cassidy? Instead, she shifted Cleopatra once again in her arms and received another growl of warning.

A voice murmured in her ear, "I've already interrogated the cat."

Savannah whirled to face Cassidy. He was wearing a pale peach shirt of the fine cotton that he favored and a gray silk tie with a perfectly executed Windsor knot. He was freshly shaven and well rested, and his smile held nothing but his usual trace of well-schooled cynicism.

Savannah's heart leaped to her throat and she didn't know whether to fling her arms around him in joy, or to throw the cat at him. Better judgment and an empathy for all defenseless creatures persuaded her to hold on to the cat.

Greg Walker did not seem surprised to see him. He demanded, "Well?"

With every ounce of determination Savannah possessed, she coolly turned her back on C. J. Cassidy, despite the fact that she would have given several years of her life to see his expression when she did so. Cassidy's voice betrayed absolutely no change of expression when he replied.

"The security camera was disabled at 1:45 a.m.," he said. "Until then, everything was normal. The necklace was in the box, just as Mrs. Bouvier and the guard reported, at eight o'clock. By 2:30 a.m. the camera was back on line, showing everything normal again. So obviously, the theft took place between 1:45 and 2:30 this morning."

Detective Jenkins, who didn't let anything get past him, inquired, "Why did it take so long?"

Savannah had to look at Cassidy then. He shrugged. "It's a complicated system. It would take some time to get it up again."

Jenkins frowned. "But not too complicated to be disabled by an amateur."

"I never said it was an amateur, Detective."

Stan Keller said, "You know that system inside and out."

The look Stan forced on Cassidy was cold and deliberate. Cassidy responded to it with a friendly smile and an easy, "I should. I designed it."

Emily, refusing to be left out of the drama for long, returned to Savannah and scooped up the cat. "It's all my fault! I *knew* I shouldn't have let that necklace out of my sight. I should have kept it here, with me, where it would still be right now if I hadn't put it in the safe."

Cassidy stepped forward, his face grave. "It would appear you're right, Mrs. Bouvier. And I have to accept full responsibility. After all, it was I who persuaded you to put the necklace in the safe."

"Yes," Stan said coolly. "It was."

Savannah stiffened, and Mrs. Bouvier looked confused. She stroked the cat, who growled at her just as it had done to Savannah, and murmured a few soothing words. She looked up at Cassidy with a misty smile.

"I know you were only doing what you thought best, and it *is* my fault, when you get down to it. After all, people only guard what they're afraid of losing and fear puts out very bad vibrations into the cosmos. So I suppose it was inevitable the necklace should be lost, but . . ." She looked at him hopefully. "If you could possibly find it before my lunch date with Wilhelm, I would be so very grateful."

Cassidy smiled at her. "I'll do my best," he promised.

He turned to the others. "Gentlemen, I think we've disturbed Mrs. Bouvier long enough. May I suggest we continue the investigation from my office?"

Savannah wanted nothing more than to follow as the men left the suite. But by the time she had given her condolences and best reassurances to Emily Bouvier, as well as having spoken a few sympathetic words to the cat, the corridor was empty.

The door to Cassidy's suite—office, Savannah had to remind herself—was open and she walked into the middle of a heated discussion. Nonetheless, the first thing her eyes went to was the floor in front of the desk. The window was open to the sea breeze, and Cassidy was standing before it, just as he had been yesterday... looking at her, reading her thoughts.

"As far as I'm concerned, it's finished," Stan was saying, loudly enough to pull Savannah's attention away from the memories of the day before and onto the matter at hand. "What are you wasting time for when your prime suspect is standing right here?"

Greg Walker said sharply, "I think that's enough, Mr. Keller."

Stan Keller turned to him, defiance in the set of his jaw. "Mr. Walker, I've been head of security at this hotel for almost twenty years. I think you'd be grateful for my expertise on a situation as serious as this. And my expertise is telling me right now there's only one man who could have pulled this job and you all know who I mean."

There was an awful, pulse-stopping silence. Greg Walker looked uncomfortable as he tried to direct his gaze toward anything but Cassidy. Detective Jenkins's face was sober. And Cassidy, when Savannah returned her eyes to him, was still looking at her with a thoughtful, absorbed expression that seemed to suggest he had not heard anything Stan had said.

Stan went on intrepidly, "The man's a known criminal—he brags about being the best in the business, for God's sake. He talked you into taking out a perfectly good security system so that he could put in his own, didn't he? He barely got it in in time, as a matter of fact. And isn't it convenient that his suite is right down the hall from Emily Bouvier's? It wouldn't be much trouble at all for him to watch her comings and goings—even without a high-tech monitoring system. We all saw the way he looked at that necklace yesterday. There wasn't a doubt in my mind—"

"All right, Stan, we get the idea." Jenkins sounded a little weary. He looked at Cassidy. "He's right, you know. Any one of those things would put you at the top of my list."

Cassidy dragged his gaze away from Savannah's with a little frown, as though he was annoyed at being distracted. He turned to Jenkins politely. "You're both right, of course. I would be my prime suspect, too. You're welcome to search my suite."

"We already have," Jenkins replied perfunctorily.

Cassidy lifted an eyebrow.

"Not," Jenkins went on smoothly, " that you would be that careless. We're also searching every vacant room in the hotel . . . just in case."

"I'm flattered by your faith in me," Cassidy murmured.

Jenkins inclined his head. "Then you'll understand why I have to ask you where you were this morning between one and three?"

Savannah stared at Jenkins, then at Cassidy, and she couldn't believe what she was hearing. But it was inevitable, wasn't it? Why should anybody give him the benefit of the doubt? Why should anyone trust him? Why should anyone believe anything he said?

That knowledge was clear in his eyes, a kind of controlled acceptance of the trap he could feel closing in, though perhaps no one but Savannah could see it. His expression remained smooth and so did his tone as he replied, "I was asleep, of course, where any decent person would be that time of night."

Jenkins nodded. "No one can substantiate that, I'm sure."

And that was when Savannah heard a voice say, "Actually, someone can."

The voice was hers.

Four pairs of male eyes fastened on her, and Savannah took a step forward. "Cassidy was with me last night," she said, "All night."

The reactions of the four men were varied and intense. Greg Walker's face reflected nothing but shock. A puzzled, almost dismayed frown shot across Jenkins's face and Stan Keller looked utterly nonplussed. But it was Cassidy's expression that affected Savannah the most, and that was the least dramatic. Nothing registered upon his face at all except a slight hardening of his jaw, a darkening of his eyes. He was furious.

Then Stan Keller sputtered, "That—that doesn't mean anything! He could have rigged that tape to make it look like the robbery took place any time he pleased. As for what she says..."

"Careful, Mr. Keller," warned Walker in a low tone.

Cassidy relaxed his shoulders with an effort and turned his attention away from Savannah once again and onto the others. "Once more, I'm afraid Mr. Keller is right, and Ms. Monterey has sullied her reputation to no avail. If I had wanted to steal the necklace, I could have done so despite all evidence to the contrary. Unfortunately for your investigation, however—" he smiled at Detective Jenkins "—I didn't."

"And also unfortunately," added Jenkins, "or maybe fortunately for you, it does take a little thing like evidence to make an arrest. So, Keller, if that's all you have, we need to move on. I'll assign one of my men to help you conduct employee interviews. I wish I had more manpower to spare but I just don't, so I'll need to rely on your staff to help search the utility areas of the hotel."

As he spoke, he was walking toward the door, the other two men following him. Greg Walker glanced over his shoulder. "Ms. Monterey?"

She felt pinned by Cassidy's gaze, unable to move even if she had wanted to. Her throat was scratchy, her voice a little hoarse. "In a minute."

She felt her boss's hesitancy, but he left with the others, closing the door behind him.

"Why," demanded Cassidy in a voice that could have frozen water, "did you do that?"

"Just being unpredictable," Savannah replied.

He snapped, "Thank you for your trouble, but I've been taking care of myself for quite some time now. There was absolutely no reason for you to get involved."

Savannah stepped forward and slapped him across the face.

He took a startled step backward, not so much from the force of her blow as from sheer surprise. And Savannah had the satisfaction of seeing the cold anger in his face wiped away by a mixture of amazement and disbelief.

"That," she told him, her eyes blazing, "is for not showing up last night. As for my getting involved—I already *am* involved with you, hadn't you noticed? I thought I made that fairly clear yesterday afternoon. Where *were* you last night? How dare you stand me up!"

Cassidy dropped his eyes, rubbing the side of his face where the faint pink imprint of her hand showed. "Savannah, don't do this. You know..."

"What I know," she said tightly, "is that I waited six hours for you to show up last night. What were *you* doing all that time?"

He looked at her again, his eyes as smooth as glass. "Stealing the necklace, obviously."

Savannah's hands closed into fists. "Now, you listen to me, C. J. Cassidy," she said darkly. "I'm in no mood to play games. So give me an answer. Why didn't you show up last night?"

Cassidy looked at her for a long moment, fighting to shore up the defenses he could feel crumbling with every breath. She looked frail and vulnerable with her hair loose around her waist and the faint bruises of sleeplessness beneath her eyes, her face devoid of makeup. Yet she was oddly formidable with her fists closed and her eyes churning. Cassidy had already learned that, in all the ways that mattered, she was much stronger than he was. That was only one of the things he found so fresh and exciting about her, so difficult to resist...so easy to love.

He had lied to her. He had kept her waiting for him last night when he had no intention of keeping their date, and yet she had come here this morning and defended him against his accusers, lied for him, possibly kept him from going to jail. Damn her for that. Damn *him* for letting it get this far, for not being able to stay away from her....

He said, "Listen to me, Savannah. You're looking at a man who stole his first car when he was fourteen years old just for the thrill of it. For the rush, for the excitement, for the danger, for the satisfaction of cheating and getting away with it. That's me, that's the kind of man I am, and you've got no business getting tangled up with someone like that."

"Why don't you let *me* decide what my business is?"

"Damn it, Savannah, don't you understand? All you see is the excitement—a man who lives on the edge but still manages to stay straight. Don't you see that living on the edge means I could slip at any minute, and it's not over for me? You think I'm reformed— sometimes even I think I'm reformed—but am I? All it takes is one slip, one temptation I can't resist, and I never know when that temptation is going to come. I never know if I'm going to walk away—or go right back to doing what I *really* do best. And you'll never know, either. That's why I can never belong to your world. And that's why I didn't show up last night."

She said, "You didn't show up last night because you were afraid. You use your past like a club to scare people away, to keep them on guard around you, and you like it when people don't trust you. As long as no one believes in you or depends on you, you don't have to be responsible for anyone but yourself, isn't that right? You always have an out. But when it started to look as though *I* might trust you, I might get close to you, it scared the hell out of you. So you made sure I wouldn't trust you—and damn near got yourself arrested in the process! Well, guess what, Cassidy? No one is going to tell me how I can or cannot feel or who I can or cannot trust, not even you. And *that's* why I gave you an alibi for last night—just to make sure you knew I don't scare off that easily.''

And with that, she turned on her heel to go. She looked back angrily. ''And another thing. Just in case you're wondering, you don't ever have to worry about not passing the temptation test again. You did that yesterday, when you held that necklace in your hands—and gave it back. You might be able to keep on convincing other people you're a bad seed, but you'll never be able to fool yourself into believing that again. Or me, either.''

She slammed the door with a force that jarred a picture on the wall, and Cassidy just stood there for a long time, staring at it. A thoughtful, disturbed frown puckered his forehead as he turned away at last, walked over to the window and looked out at the sea.

Nine

The remainder of the day passed in a nightmarish blur and by four o'clock Savannah knew what it must be like to be mayor of a city under siege. A hotel was like a small city in that it supported everything from merchants to a playground, and not one department was unaffected by the crisis. Though technically Greg Walker was in charge, it seemed to Savannah that more than a fair share had landed on her desk.

Savannah was generally at her best in a crisis. Never before had she failed to rise to the occasion or in any way entertained the possibility of shirking her duty. But today she found herself looking at defeat. She simply wasn't up to the job.

Detective Jenkins had once told her that if a crime like this wasn't solved within the first six hours, the chances of solving it at all decreased exponentially with every hour thereafter. And it didn't take a detective to realize that if the necklace ever left the island, the chances against recovery doubled instantly. As far as any of them knew, the necklace had already been passed into the hands of some fence and was even now being broken up for resale. The thought made Savannah feel ill.

She was not kept apprised of the progress of the investigation. She was too busy fielding phone calls from irate employees and alarmed guests, who demanded to know why the place was suddenly swarming with uniforms. She squashed rumors that ranged from a murder on the premises to an outbreak of Legionnaires' disease. She persuaded the chef *not* to walk off the job in the middle of the lunch rush and talked the prince of a small but incredibly wealthy nation into not canceling the reservation he had made for his family.

And she managed all this with a heart that was breaking and a spirit that was drained.

She did not hear a word from Cassidy. For all she knew, he might have been carried off in cuffs by now. What, exactly, she expected to hear from him, she wasn't sure, but after the emotional scene that morning, surely she deserved something. Surely he had something to say to her. Surely he *felt* something.

Or perhaps not. Perhaps she had been entirely wrong about him. Perhaps she would have been better off to leave the wild reckless impulses to people like her parents and her sisters, who knew how to deal with them better than she did. Wouldn't it be ironic—and somehow fitting—if the first and only completely impulsive thing she had ever done was to fall in love with the wrong man?

Emily Bouvier was enjoying the excitement almost as much as she mourned the loss of the necklace; besides, the necklace had been fully insured. Every half hour, she managed to tear herself away from the heart of the investigation to call Savannah with an update or a complaint. It had taken all of the persuasive powers of the police, Greg Walker and Savannah to keep her from calling a press conference; trying to keep her from telling her many friends the entire story was becoming a study in never-ending vigilance.

It all combined to form a tidal wave of impossibility that swamped Savannah with defeat. She couldn't do everything. She didn't want to do everything. None of this was her problem and she couldn't deal with it any longer.

So at four o'clock she picked up her purse, locked her office door and left.

"Call the switchboard," she told her secretary. "Tell them not to put any calls through to Emily Bouvier or let any calls from her leave the hotel."

Holly's eyes rounded. "But you can't—"

"I can and I am," snapped Savannah. "That's the only way to keep her harmless gossip from bringing the press down on us. If that happens, we'll never locate the necklace."

Again, her secretary stared at her. "You don't think . . . could it still be in the hotel?"

"Probably not," Savannah admitted tiredly, "but since that's our best chance of recovering it, I'd like to hope it is. Anyway, just tell the switchboard to keep Mrs. Bouvier in isolation overnight—have them tell her it's a technical problem and they're trying to fix it. That's the best I can do. That's *all* I can do. And if I don't get out of here right now, I'll be stuck for the rest of the night, so I'm going home. You do the same when you've made that call."

"Thanks." Already she was dialing the switchboard.

She left by way of the front door, just as she was accustomed to doing, only today a plainclothes security guard blocked her way. She noted with approval that Stan had at least been smart enough not to have the extra security he had brought in wear uniforms. She nodded to the young man and tried to move around him, but once again he blocked her way.

"You weren't thinking of leaving the building, were you, ma'am?" he inquired a little hesitantly.

She stared at him. "As a matter of fact, I was. I try to do so at least once a day. What is going on here?"

He swallowed hard, looking uncomfortable. "I'm sorry, ma'am. I have orders not to let any employee leave the building."

"Do you have any idea who I am?"

He looked even more miserable. He knew who she was from her name tag. "I'm sorry, ma'am. I was told the orders especially applied to you."

Her incredulity grew, as well as her outrage. At the end of a day like the one she had just had, this was all she needed. "Who told you that?" she demanded. "Whose orders are these? The police? Stan Keller?"

"Actually...the order came from Mr. Cassidy. I could call up there if you like and—"

But he had to call out the last part of his offer because Savannah, moving with the impetus of fury, was already halfway to the elevator bank.

Her anger had not abated by the time she reached the third floor, which was in much the same state of chaos in which she had left it earlier that day. The door to the Bouvier suite was open and Savannah smothered a groan as she saw, in the few seconds it took her to pass the room, two people enter and three leave. Cleopatra was in the hallway, helping herself to leftovers from one of the three room-service trays stacked on the cart outside the door. She winced as she heard Emily's shrill voice demand, "What do you mean you can't place that call?"

The sense of helplessness and frustration only added to her anger at Cassidy, misdirected though it might be, as she marched to the door and knocked loudly.

When he didn't answer quickly enough, she banged on the door with her fist again and shouted, "Cassidy! Open up!"

She drew back her fist to knock again when the door swung open and she almost lost her balance. He stepped back and she glared at him as she pushed her way inside.

"Just what do you think you're doing?" she demanded. "Are you crazy? I certainly hope you don't think you can hold people hostage in this hotel forever, because sooner or later—"

"Actually," he said, closing the door firmly behind them, "you're the only one I wanted to hold hostage."

Savannah whirled with more angry words on her lips but they died unspoken as she looked at him fully for the first time. With his shirtsleeves rolled up, his hair tousled and his beard-shadow darker than usual, he was sexy enough to stop her thoughts in midformation and wipe away every trace of the anger that had propelled her thus far. But it wasn't just his appearance that took her breath away. It was his smile, gentle and tender and just a little bit mysterious, mesmeric and compelling and completely irresistible.

Savannah stood where she was and cautiously watched him approach.

"I promised you the best adventure you ever had," he reminded her, "and it's not over yet."

He took her into his arms and Savannah felt herself begin to melt. His fingers cupped her neck, his face moved close to hers. Surrender began to creep through every cell of her body.

And then she caught a glimpse of something over his shoulder, a sparkle of something caught in a drawer hastily half-closed. She knew in an instant what it was.

Emily Bouvier's necklace.

Ten

Savannah pushed him roughly away and crossed the room with her heart pounding in her chest. A faint and helpless little voice inside her was crying, *No, don't let it be!* while another one shouted harshly, *Of course it is, you fool, you should have known better than to trust him! You should have known...*

She jerked upon the drawer and pulled out the necklace.

The diamonds winked in the sunlight as the necklace draped through her fingers; the emerald gleamed with inner fire. Its brash seductive beauty seemed to mock her, yet it held her captive in its spell. Her throat dried up. She couldn't move. She could only stare, helpless and hopeless, as Cassidy came toward her.

Ultimately he stopped before her, so close she was sure she could hear the slamming of her heart. So close his presence seemed to swallow her, his warmth and his scent invading her.

She looked up at him, hoping to see something there that could make it all go away, or at least make her understand. Regret, sorrow, shame—something. She saw nothing but a kind of guarded waiting, a cautious curiosity.

She said, "I don't believe it." Those were not the words she meant to say, but those were the words that came out. "I can't believe you did this."

And he said with a careful, watchful tone, "Believe I did what, Savannah?"

"Damn you." Her voice was shaking, and she had to close her fingers around the necklace to keep from dropping it.

Cassidy said gently, "Now, angel, you don't really think I stole that necklace, do you?"

Savannah looked at him helplessly. Did she? How could she not? The man was a professional thief, he had been caught red-handed, of *course* she believed he had stolen it. And yet...

She cried, "For God's sake, Cassidy what do you expect from me? I don't want to believe it, I wish I didn't have to believe it—"

"Then don't."

He reached out his hand and loosened the necklace from her fingers. Helplessly, she let him take it, thinking frantically. "Listen," she said. "It might not be too late. If we can get it back to her room, you know how flighty Mrs. Bouvier is—if I can distract her while you—''

He smiled tenderly. "You'd do that for me?"

"Cassidy, please!'' She gasped and stepped back as he unfastened the necklace and made as though to slip it around her neck. "What are you doing?"

He answered softly, "Just a little something to make up for all the things I've stolen from you."

Savannah's knees went weak and her head actually swam as he lifted his arms and fastened the necklace around her neck. The stones were warm from his body heat as they settled against her skin, the smooth hard shape of the necklace surprisingly light, oddly sensuous.

Savannah couldn't move. Her voice barely managed a croak as she said, "Cassidy, this isn't funny. We've got to get this back where it belongs before someone finds out."

His smile deepened. "Relax," he assured her. "No one has any use for this necklace except me. It's a paste imitation," he told her. "I'm afraid they haven't found the real one yet."

Savannah stared at him. The weight of the necklace was solid and real, the smile in his eyes just as real. For a moment, just a moment, she wavered. Was he telling the truth? Could she live with herself if she found out he wasn't?

Could she live with herself if she refused to believe him now, after they had come so far? A moment ago she had been willing to lie, cheat and be a conspirator in crime to help him replace the necklace before he was found out. How could she doubt him now when he claimed his innocence with such simple conviction?

But in the end she believed him because she loved him, and she wanted to believe him more than anything in the world.

She sank heavily to a chair, her fingers closing around the stones at her neck. It was a long time before she could speak, and all the time she could feel Cassidy watching her, his gaze alert, wondering how deep her trust in him went.

Finally she muttered, "I could strangle you, for scaring me so."

Cassidy relaxed. "That wasn't the reaction I was hoping for." He lifted his hand and cupped her chin, tilting her face upward. His eyes were lit with tenderness and admiration. "It looks magnificent on you," he said. "It looks the way it was meant to look—a work of art, complimenting a work of art."

Savannah fingered the necklace a little self-consciously, but she could feel her face warming with his praise, her heart speeding. "Cassidy..."

His expression grew serious, and his voice was quiet. "I'm sorry if I worried you, angel. But I couldn't let you leave here today thinking...well, thinking I didn't care. You believed in me." He dropped his eyes. "I'm not sure anyone has ever done that before."

With his words the anger that had sustained her, melted away, to be replaced by a much simpler, much truer emotion. "I couldn't help believing in you," she answered softly. "I love you, you know."

His eyes met hers again. His hand drifted down to cover hers on the necklace. "You were right in everything you said about me this morning. I set you up last night—I figured it would be easier on you if you discovered what a louse I was firsthand . . . and easier for me, because I was far too close to falling in love with you. No, I take that back. I was already in love with you. Hopelessly, foolishly in love . . . and *that's* the most dangerous thing I've ever done."

Savannah didn't know who made the first move and it didn't matter. They came together like the tide seeking the shore, like earth and sky, naturally, inevitably, and on a single breath. Savannah lifted her arms to his neck and he bent to meet her, pulling her to her feet. Their lips met. Dizziness swirled and fever surged as he placed an arm beneath her knees and swept her off her feet and into his arms.

They tumbled to the bed together, limbs entwined, bodies straining, heartbeats seeking a single rhythm. Savannah tasted the stubble of his beard and the smooth hot texture of his neck. She pushed his shirt off his shoulders and stretched upward to place long and lingering kisses on his shoulders, his chest, encircling his flat brown nipples with her tongue. She saw the pleasure of her caresses suffuse his face and a spiral of ecstasy traveled outward from the pit of her stomach, from nothing more than watching his eyes.

The late-afternoon light filtered through the sheer curtains and painted moving shadows across the walls, as tenderly, punctuating each movement with a caress or a kiss, Cassidy removed her clothes. His tongue traced a slow exquisite pattern from the pounding pulse in her throat to the sensitive dip just below her sternum. She gasped out loud in pleasure as his mouth returned to her breasts, encircling each nipple by turn with his tongue, drawing gently, sending frissons of pure pleasure deep into the center of her womb. And just when she thought she could not bear the need for him another moment, when it seemed the very cells of her skin cried out for him, he entered her, and rapture blossomed inside her.

Their lovemaking was fierce and joyous and unrestrained, pushing the boundaries of anything either of them had known before. Pleasure was attenuated to its finest, purest extension, then dissolved into something more intense than pleasure, grander than the mere physical. Fulfillment bloomed and cascaded within them and between them, shaking the world around them and sealing them together, united and strong, forever.

When heartbeats and breaths finally began to resume their normal rhythms, when the glow of physical wonder began to change into a deeper contentment, Savannah shifted her head against his shoulder and murmured, "We really have to stop carrying on like this during working hours."

She lay naked in his arms atop the tangled bed covers, wearing nothing but the emerald necklace. Cassidy smiled because this was the first time he had realized that she was still wearing it. He carefully ran his fingers through the damp hair that framed her face, combing out the long strands behind her, marveling at the beauty of its color and texture.

"Who needs emeralds?" he murmured and kissed her lips. "As for the way we carry on . . ." He placed another kiss on her left temple. "I can't promise to stop it completely, but I can just about promise you this will be the last time during working hours. Unless I miss my guess, in fact, this will be the last hour of my employment at your hotel."

Savannah propped herself up on her elbow to look at him, disturbed. "Cassidy, you're not expecting trouble, are you? Is there something I should know?"

He touched the tip of her chin with his index finger, smiling. "Do you mean besides how entranced I am by you? How utterly bewitched? How you've changed my life and everything about it in the twinkling of an eye?"

Savannah couldn't hold back a smile of her own, as much as she tried to remain stern. A two-million-dollar necklace was still missing and that was no laughing matter, yet it seemed to Savannah, as she lay wrapped in his warmth and looked into his eyes, a mere trifle.

"That's what I like about you," she replied. "Life with you is never dull."

"That I can promise you." He kissed her again, with a slow and lingering tenderness that breathed new life into the glowing embers of passion. "The first, I hope, of many promises," he added gently and drew her more snugly into his arms.

Savannah settled against him contentedly. Although she no longer cared about the answer, she reminded him, "You didn't answer my question."

"The security system is in place, and the burglary case is on the verge of being solved. Once you have your thief, I will have fulfilled my contract and the hotel will have no more use for my services."

Once again, she got up on one elbow to look at him, her curiosity aroused. "What do you mean, the case is on the verge of being solved? Do you know something...wait a minute." Her hand flew to the necklace at her throat. "You have a plan! You're going to use this copy to catch the thief!"

He smiled and sat up. "Right. And it's about time to put that plan into motion."

"What do you mean, it's about time?" Incredulity made her voice rise. "This place has been a madhouse all day! Are you telling me that you—"

She broke off with a gasp as a heavy weight landed on her thighs. Cleopatra the cat glared at her and hissed.

"Well, hello there." Cassidy reached forward and scratched the cat behind the ears. "Where did you come from?"

"She was mooching off the room-service tray in the hall." Savannah said impatiently. "She must have come in when you opened the door for me."

"Well then." Cassidy stroked the cat under the chin. "We'd better get her back home, don't you think?"

"Cassidy—"

"Forgive me, angel, but I'm afraid I have to take it back." He reached forward and unclasped the necklace from Savannah's neck. "It's the last time, I promise."

Savannah watched in growing disbelief as he wrapped the necklace several times around the cat's neck, like a collar, and fastened it securely. "It wasn't my intention to keep everyone in suspense," he explained as he did so. "I knew Mrs. Bouvier had a copy made— her insurance company insisted upon it. Of course, the intention was that she should display the copy and keep the real necklace under lock and key, but we know her reaction to that. I had to wait for the copy to get here before I could put my plan in motion."

He released Cleopatra and she bounded to the floor with a yowl. He stood and began pulling on his clothes, tossing a grin at her over his shoulder. "The real excitement is about to begin, and I've reserved a front-row seat for you. And although, to me, you couldn't look more delectable..." His eyes moved over her figure with a slow appreciation that made her skin tingle. "You might want to consider dressing more appropriately."

Five minutes later, Savannah was hopping on one foot as she tried to get her shoe on while hurrying to follow Cassidy to the door. She didn't like the idea of leaving this room, and for more than one reason. One look at her face and any stranger would be able to tell what she and Cassidy had been doing, and why should she want to hide it? She wanted to shout it to the world.

"For heaven's sake," she complained breathlessly, "what's the hurry? You've waited all day!"

"One thing I've learned in my many years of working both sides of the fence," he replied, "is that time and the law wait for no man."

He scooped up Cleopatra, who hissed at him roundly, and added, "Jenkins works an eight-hour shift. He'll be leaving the hotel in another ten minutes."

Savannah crowded close to him as he opened the door to the hallway. "What are you doing, anyway? What's your plan?"

He dropped Cleopatra into the hallway. "There you go, nice kitty," he murmured. "Go to mama."

"What—"

"Shh."

And to make certain his admonishment was obeyed, he covered her mouth with his own.

The shriek that came from the suite down the hall tore them apart. It no doubt did the same to couples three stories above them.

"Cleopatra, darling! You found it, you wonderful cat! You found it!"

Cassidy opened the door a crack and peeked through. Savannah crowded in close behind to get a glimpse.

He nodded in satisfaction at the site of people scurrying through the hall, some in uniforms and some not. "Let's give everyone a few minutes to get up here, shall we?"

"I don't understand," Savannah said. "Doesn't Mrs. Bouvier know it's a copy? Didn't you tell her?"

"Of course not. Would you trust her with a secret like that? I had her secretary send for it."

"But why? What—"

He turned away from the door, laying a finger lightly across her lips. "The plan," he told her, "is to make the thief think the necklace has been recovered. The first thing he'll do is check his hiding place. And we, with any luck, will be right behind him."

Savannah's eyes grew round as she breathed, "This *is* an adventure." Then she clutched at his sleeve in sudden consternation. "There won't be any shooting, will there?"

His face broke into a grin and he kissed her quickly on the lips. "I do adore you." He turned back to the door.

"But how will you know who to follow?" She pressed close, trying to get a better look. "There are dozens of people coming and going!"

"Angel," he replied patiently, "we know who the thief is. I've known since the day after I got here, as a matter of fact. And you surely don't think I'd design a security system that could be disabled by an amateur, do you? The back-up cameras kicked in the minute the primary system went off-line, and we have it all on tape—all except one little detail. Where he hid the necklace."

Savannah sank back, staring at him. "That's why Detective Jenkins didn't arrest you!"

He smiled tenderly. "You really did sacrifice yourself for nothing this morning. I'd already shown him the tape. But for the sake of the hotel—and Mrs. Bouvier, of course—we decided to give my plan to recover the necklace a chance to work before making an arrest."

Savannah's head was swimming. "But—who was it? Who stole the necklace?"

"There," Cassidy said quietly, and directed Savannah's attention to the man who was just getting on the elevator. "That's the man."

And as she stared, stunned, at the person he indicated, the elevator doors closed and Cassidy caught her hand. "Come on," he said, tugging her along. "We've got a thief to catch."

"But I don't understand." After running two flights down, Savannah was gasping. "Why? Why would a man like him *do* this?"

"He had a gambling problem none of you ever knew about," Cassidy replied quietly. He was barely winded as he opened the service-stairs door a crack and peered through. "It only started to get out of hand recently, thus the burglaries. As for the necklace—I don't think he ever intended anything so ambitious. He probably doesn't have the first idea how to dispose of it now that he's got it. I'd guess a good eighty percent of the motive was to prove that he could—it hits you like that sometimes. The other twenty percent was probably to discredit me. With me out of the way, it'd be a lot easier to continue the burglaries during the tourist season."

"Incredible," Savannah murmured.

He lifted a hand for silence and closed the door without a sound. He spoke into the walkie-talkie he took from his pocket. "It looks like the west wing utility closet," he said softly. "He just went in."

He turned off the radio and repocketed it. He turned to Savannah. In the bright fluorescent lighting, every line and plane of his face was clear, and it was the most beautiful face Savannah had ever seen.

The expression in his eyes was quiet and sober as he said, "Savannah, there's one more thing I have to thank you for. This morning, when you said I'd passed the test when I gave that necklace back to Mrs. Bouvier yesterday—you were right. I don't know that I would have done anything differently if you hadn't been there, but I never would have *known* what I would do if it hadn't been for you. I guess what I'm trying to say is—you not only believed in me, you made me believe in myself." He cupped her face in his hand, stroking her cheek with his forefinger. "How do you thank a person for something like that?"

Savannah smiled up at him, turning her cheek briefly into his caress. "I'll think of something," she answered. "I promise."

After a moment, reluctantly, he dropped his hand and turned back to the door, opening it silently. "You'd better stay here," he whispered, "just in case."

"Oh, no." She pressed close to him. "I'm staying with you."

And when he turned a look on her that was filled with argument, she cut him off by saying stubbornly, "The adventure isn't over, and you promised. Remember?"

He released a breath that ended in a rueful smile. "I remember. Stay behind me. And be quiet."

They moved silently down the tiled service corridor toward the door marked Utility. The kitchen wasn't far away and the muted sounds of pots and pans, voices and activity reached them. Otherwise, there was nothing.

Cassidy put his hand on the doorknob. He looked at her as though to question her readiness. With a surge of excitement that escalated her heartbeat, Savannah nodded. She thought if she lived to be a hundred, she would never forget this, their first case together.

Cassidy opened the door.

Stan Keller turned, a look of utter shock on his face. On the shelf beside him was an empty cardboard box. A ceiling tile had been removed over his head. In his hand was the emerald necklace.

"Ingenious," commented Cassidy. "It would have taken us days to search the crawl spaces. By then, you would have been gone."

In swift succession, a dozen or more emotions crossed Stan's face—anger, defiance, frustration, panic. He made a move as though to lunge at them and Cassidy swiftly flung out his arm, shielding Savannah and pushing her behind him.

The firm voice of authority stopped Stan cold.

"Forget it, Keller. It's over."

Detective Jenkins stood beside them while two of his officers pushed forward to cuff Stan.

"All right, Cassidy," he said as he watched the proceedings. "I'll give you this one. But I want you to know I never really took you off my suspect list."

Cassidy grinned and slipped his arm around Savannah's waist. "You're a wise man, my friend," he answered, "but you overlooked one thing."

"Oh?" Jenkins's tone was skeptical, and his eyes made particular note of the way Cassidy looked at Savannah. "What's that?"

"I'm not working alone anymore. And I'm reformed." He smiled at Savannah. "For good, this time."

Savannah laid her head against Cassidy's shoulder and enjoyed the look of worried disapproval that crossed the detective's face.

"Better get used to it, Detective," she advised. "I have a feeling you're going to be seeing a lot more of Mr. Cassidy. After all, the position of head of security at this hotel appears to be open, and I do the hiring."

Jenkins looked at her for a moment as though uncertain whether or not she was joking. Then he grunted noncommittally and turned away to watch the officer lead Stan down the hall. Another officer stopped to give him the cardboard box with the necklace inside.

Jenkins opened the box, took out the necklace and held it up to the light. "Damned if I can see the difference," he remarked. "Here you go, Cassidy." And to Savannah's utter astonishment, he tossed the necklace to Cassidy. "A little souvenir."

Cassidy caught the necklace one-handed, grinning.

"Drop by the station when you get a chance and give us a statement," Jenkins said, and followed his officers out.

Savannah said, "Come on, let's get the necklace back to Mrs. Bouvier where it belongs. It makes me nervous just being this close to it." She tugged at his arm, but he hesitated.

"Actually," he said. "Mrs. Bouvier already has her necklace."

Savannah stepped back, staring at the necklace in his hand. "But wait a minute. I thought you said the other necklace..." Her eyes grew wide and her voice hoarsened as she looked from the necklace to his face. "Which one is real?"

His grin turned a little sheepish. "I guess I colored the facts a little before. You don't really think I'd leave a necklace worth two million dollars in a ceiling crawl space for anyone to find, do you?"

Her throat was dry. "Then you knew where it was all along?"

"Not all along," Cassidy confessed. "And it was important to catch Stan with the goods."

Savannah swallowed hard. "You let me wear—a two-million-dollar necklace?" She swallowed again. "You let a *cat* wear it?"

"You are worth every penny," he assured her. "The cat..." He shrugged. "That's still open for debate."

Smiling, he lifted his arms and fastened the necklace around her neck. "Value," he told her, "is a relative thing. That's something else you taught me."

Savannah sank back against the door frame weakly. "You," she said, "are impossible."

"I certainly hope so. I don't want to get *too* reformed."

Laughing softly, Savannah went into his arms. "Somehow, I don't think there's much danger of that."

Cassidy kissed her hair. "Let's go home."

She slipped her arm around his waist as they started down the corridor. "To your suite?"

"A hotel is not a home. At least—" he looked at her meaningfully, "—I hope it won't be much longer."

She pretended to think about that. "You have a Jacuzzi," she reminded him.

"But you have a garden."

Savannah's smile was secret and content as she rested her head on his shoulder. "So I do," she said. "Let's go home."

* * * * *

▼ SILHOUETTE
Desire

COMING NEXT MONTH

LUCY AND THE STONE Dixie Browning

Man of the Month

Stone McCloud believed all the rumours about scandalous Lucy Dooley—until he went to Coronoke Island determined to thwart her plans. But who was hoodwinking whom?

PERSISTENT LADY Jackie Merritt

Saxon Brothers

Cash Saxon's arrival to take over Augusta Parrish's logging company was unannounced, unexpected and completely *unwanted*. So was the intense passion that sizzled between them!

BOTHERED Jennifer Greene

The Connor Men

Samantha Adams was *every* man's fantasy—beautiful, sensual and uninhibited. But Seth Connor was tempted to run for the hills...

THE TROUBLE WITH CAASI Debbie Macomber

Caasi hadn't noticed Blake Sherrill's lean good looks until he resigned, but suddenly he was all she could think about. How could she make him stay?

ONCE UPON A FULL MOON Helen R. Myers

Worth Drury seemed to be playing guardian angel to street urchin Roxanne Grimes. But was he really just a devil in disguise?

WISH UPON A STARR Nancy Martin

Jack Patterson only believed in what he could see, and it took sexy psychic Christie Starr to teach him to trust his instincts!

COMING NEXT MONTH FROM

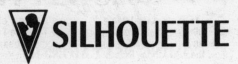 **SILHOUETTE**

Sensation

*A thrilling mix of passion, adventure
and drama*

HOLDING OUT FOR A HERO Marie Ferrarella
BORN TO BE BAD Naomi Horton
CHEROKEE THUNDER Rachel Lee
SOMEWHERE OUT THERE Emilie Richards

Intrigue

*Danger, deception and desire—
new from Silhouette...*

SHADOW OF A DOUBT Margaret Chittenden
TO DIE FOR M J Rodgers
KEEPING SECRETS Jasmine Cresswell
TORCH JOB Patricia Rosemoor

Special Edition

Satisfying romances packed with emotion

JUST HOLD ON TIGHT! Andrea Edwards
DANGEROUS ALLIANCE Lindsay McKenna
A VOW TO LOVE Sherryl Woods
MAN OF THE MOUNTAIN Christine Rimmer
WILD IS THE WIND Laurie Paige
THAT OUTLAW ATTITUDE Noreen Brownlie

Win a year's supply of Silhouette Sensations

ABSOLUTELY FREE!

YES! you could win a whole year's supply of Silhouette Sensations by playing the Treasure Trail Game. Its simple! - there are seven separate items of treasure hidden on the island, follow the instructions for each and when you arrive at the final square, work out their grid positions, (i.e **D4**) and fill in the grid reference boxes.

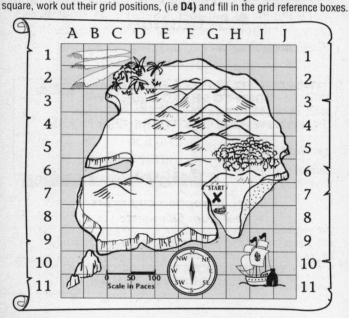

From the start, walk 250 paces to the *North*.

GRID REFERENCE

Now turn *West* and walk 150 paces.

GRID REFERENCE

From this position walk 150 paces *South*.

GRID REFERENCE

Now take 100 paces *East*.

GRID REFERENCE

Then 100 *South*.

GRID REFERENCE

And finally 50 paces *East*.

GRID REFERENCE

Please turn over for entry details

SEND YOUR ENTRY
NOW!

The first five correct entries picked out of the bag after the closing date will each win one year's supply of Silhouette Sensations (four books every month for twelve months - worth over £90). What could be easier?

Don't forget to enter your name and address in the space below, then put this page in an envelope and post it today (you don't need a stamp).

Competition closes 31st March '95.

TREASURE TRAIL competition
FREEPOST
P.O. Box 236
Croydon
Surrey CR9 9EL

Are you a Reader Service subscriber?   Yes ☐   No ☐

Ms/Mrs/Miss/Mr _____ COMSS

Address _____

_____

_____

_____ Postcode _____

_____

Signature _____

One application per household. Offer valid only in U.K. and Eire. You may be mailed with offers from other reputable companies as a result of this application. Please tick box if you would prefer not to receive such offers. ☐